Daisy wa [illegible] **with colo** [illegible] **fierce cha** [illegible] **how her soft feminine curves had felt when he was carrying her.**

An answer came to him.

"I'll give you a job," Ethan said.

Her eyes widened in astonishment, then narrowed with suspicion. "What as? Your cleaning lady?"

There was a huge appeal in that image—Daisy on her hands and knees, scrubbing his floors, her perky bottom swaying with the action. But he knew he was dead if he suggested it.

"If I have to clean floors, I will, but they won't be yours," she vowed rebelliously.

"How about housekeeper?" The fight in her eyes wavered into a sea of vulnerable uncertainty—the need for no break in her income warring with a mountain of doubts about what she might be getting into by putting herself in his power.

"Are you serious?" she asked huskily.

"Yes."

Once they'd settled on a meeting at the house at eight o'clock on Monday morning of the next week, she took her leave of him, very firmly, and Ethan let her go, watching the seductive swish of her bottom, content with the thought he'd be seeing a lot more of Daisy Donahue in the very near future.

He was looking forward to it.

AT HIS
Service

From glass slippers to silk sheets

Once upon a time there was a humble housekeeper. Proud but poor, she went to work for a charming and ruthless rich man.

She thought her place was below stairs—but her gorgeous boss had other ideas.

He didn't want her in the kitchen, polishing the silver.

He didn't want her in the lounge, plumping the cushions.

He didn't want her in the library, dusting the books.

Her place was in the bedroom, between his luxurious silk sheets.

Stripped of her threadbare uniform, buxom and blushing in his bed, he'll show her a woman's work has never been so much fun!

Emma Darcy

THE BILLIONAIRE'S HOUSEKEEPER MISTRESS

AT HIS
Service

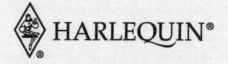

HARLEQUIN®

TORONTO • NEW YORK • LONDON
AMSTERDAM • PARIS • SYDNEY • HAMBURG
STOCKHOLM • ATHENS • TOKYO • MILAN • MADRID
PRAGUE • WARSAW • BUDAPEST • AUCKLAND

Recycling programs
for this product may
not exist in your area.

ISBN-13: 978-0-373-12942-3

THE BILLIONAIRE'S HOUSEKEEPER MISTRESS

First North American Publication 2010.

This edition published by arrangement with Harlequin Books S.A.

For questions and comments about the quality of this book please contact us at Customer_eCare@Harlequin.ca.

www.eHarlequin.com

Printed in U.S.A.

All about the author...
Emma Darcy

EMMA DARCY was born in Australia and currently lives on a beautiful country property in New South Wales. She has moved from country to city to towns and back to country, sporadically indulging her love of tropical islands with numerous vacations.

Her ambition to be an actress was partly satisfied by playing in amateur theater productions, but ultimately fulfilled in becoming a writer.

Initially a teacher of French and English, she changed her career to computer programming before marriage and motherhood settled her into a community life. Her creative urges were channeled into oil painting, pottery, designing and overseeing the construction and decorating of two homes, all in the midst of keeping up with three lively sons and the very busy social life of her businessman husband.

A voracious reader, the step to writing her own books seemed a natural progression and the challenge of creating wonderful stories was soon highly addictive. With her strong interest in people and relationships, Emma found the world of romance fiction a happy one.

Currently, she has broadened her horizons and begun to write mainstream women's fiction. Other new directions include her most recent adventures of blissfully breezing around the Gulf of Mexico from Florida to Louisiana in a red Ford Mustang convertible, and risking the perils of the tortuous road along the magnificent Amalfi Coast in Italy.

Her conviction that we must make all we can out of the life we are given keeps her striving to know more, be more, give more, and this is reflected in all her books.

CHAPTER ONE

'DARLING, can you save me?'

Daisy Donohue froze. Lynda Twiggley's distinctive drawl was unmistakeable. It pierced the general buzz of conversation from the celebrity crowd and shot a bolt of alarm down Daisy's spine. If there was any saving to be done, as Lynda's PA, she had to do it, fast and effectively, or be lashed by her employer's sharp tongue for dereliction of duty.

She snapped into action, swinging around to find the source of the problem. The VIP marquee seemed packed with tall people. A bevy of Australia's top models had been flown in to add glamour to the event, which certainly wasn't known as the Magic Millions for nothing. Everyone here was either loaded with or associated with big money and they expected everything to be perfect for them. Especially her employer.

Being only of average height, and wearing sensible low-heeled shoes for all the toing and froing her work demanded today, Daisy stretched up on tiptoe, trying to spot the spray of royal-blue feathers that sprouted from Lynda's much-prized and hideously expensive Neil Grigg hat. A few tell-tale blue arrowheads placed her target near the open bar where there shouldn't be a problem. She had already checked there were ample cases of French champagne and every other choice of drink available. Had there been some spillage on Lynda's blue silk designer outfit?

Bad, bad, bad, Daisy thought in a burst of panic, quickly elbowing her way through the millionaire melee, wondering how she was going to fix some unfixable stain. Her hammering heart was intensely relieved when she arrived on the scene and found her employer working hard at currying the favour of a man. But not just any man. As recognition hit, her heart started hammering all over again for a multitude of reasons.

This was the man reputed to have saved the richest people in Australia from suffering any nasty fall-out from the current global financial crisis—Ethan Cartwright, the whiz-kid financier who had foreseen the crash and diverted all the big cash to enterprises that would always return a profit, even in a recession.

Daisy stopped dead behind Lynda's shoulder and stared at him, a riot of emotions hitting her hard— anger, resentment, a wild hostility at the terrible injustice of the rich getting richer while the poor got poorer, especially her parents who were trapped in a debt they could no longer service. This man, above all others, represented that miserable situation.

She'd read about him, seen photographs of him, but what made her inner turmoil more savage was how stunningly handsome he really was in the flesh. The thick, wavy, black hair, twinkling green eyes, a strong male face that didn't have one unpleasing feature capping a tall, perfectly proportioned physique which carried the perfectly tailored suit he wore with distinction…it was so wickedly unfair! The man had absolutely *everything*! She doubly resented the fact that he had a sexual impact on her. And no doubt on every woman who was subjected to his power-packed presence.

It was highly disconcerting when he suddenly shifted his attention from Lynda Twiggley to shoot a quizzical look over her shoulder straight at Daisy. Had he *felt* her hostile stare? The sexy black eyebrows with their late kick upwards—just like Brad Pitt's—lifted with a kind of bemused puzzlement, and the startling green eyes bored into hers, searching for answers that pride forbade her to ever tell him.

Vexed by his distraction, Lynda swung around to deal with an unwelcome intrusion. With the recognition that no finesse was needed on a mere employee, her steely blue eyes savaged Daisy with displeasure. 'What do you want, Dee-Dee?' she snapped.

'Nothing, Ms Twiggley,' Daisy replied with as much aplomb as she could muster, given the squeamish spotlight of two sets of eyes demanding explanations. 'I thought I heard you calling for assistance.'

Lynda clicked her tongue impatiently. 'Not right now. And stop hovering. I'm sure you have more useful things to do.'

'Yes, of course. I'm sorry for interrupting. Please excuse me.'

Daisy had already begun her retreat when Ethan Cartwright intervened. 'Wait!' he commanded, stepping forward, one arm outstretched in appeal. He smiled, his perfectly sculpted mouth breaking open to show a row of perfect white teeth, making Daisy instantly deter-

mined that he wouldn't get a bite out of her, regardless
of how charming he set out to be. 'We haven't met,' he
said in a voice as rich as the rest of him. 'I would have
remembered a Dee-Dee. It's such an unusual name. Be
so kind as to introduce us, Lynda.'

'They're her initials, not her name,' Lynda said
with a tinkling laugh that had Daisy's spine crawling
with dislike for her employer and her endlessly pa-
tronising manner. If she didn't *need* this job and the
pay packet that went with it, she would have walked
out on day one when Lynda had stated she couldn't
have a PA called Daisy because she associated that
name with a lowly cow. Dee-Dee sounded far more
upmarket.

'This is my PA, Ethan,' Lynda continued in a dismissive tone. 'No one you need to know.'

The snobbish remark apparently did not sit well with
him. 'On the contrary, should I do business with you,
your PA may be my first point of contact,' he countered,
a hard glint in the green eyes.

'Oh, very well then,' Lynda conceded, realising he
was going to persist and if she wanted him to butter her
bread she had to toe his line. 'Ethan Cartwright, Daisy
Donohue.'

'A pleasure to meet you, Mr Cartwright,' Daisy
rattled out, wanting only to escape back into the crowd.

He viewed her curiously, offering his hand as
though sensing her desire to bolt and purposely delay-
ing her. 'Probably more of a pleasure for me to meet
you, Daisy Donahue,' he said, amusement dancing in
his eyes.

Oh, sure! What fun! Big man condescending to the
little brown cow, Daisy thought viciously as she took

his hand to complete the polite formality. The flesh contact tingled hotly and his grip felt aggressively strong, pressing a dominant will that she fiercely rebelled against when he held onto her hand longer than polite formality required.

'Please excuse me, Mr Cartwright. I don't have time to dally. I'm needed elsewhere,' she said firmly, tearing her gaze from the devilishly attractive green eyes and giving a subservient nod to Lynda Twiggley whose bad temper was probably already simmering at having an important conversation interrupted.

Apparently Ethan Cartwright had enough sensitivity to realise he might be causing her trouble and backed off, releasing her hand, though still smiling at her as though she pleased him, though why she would seemed totally perverse of him when the marquee was full of gorgeous women who would undoubtedly love his attention. She had brown hair, brown eyes and was wearing brown, conscious of keeping herself as insignificant as possible, not blotting one bit of the limelight her boss liked.

'If you have a spare minute, place a bet on Midas Magic,' he said on a parting note.

Put good money on a horse! Not in a million years! Daisy's tongue lost its discipline. 'Is that your best financial advice?' she shot at him in fiery scorn for all he stood for.

He laughed, giving a breathtaking oomph to his sexual magnetism. 'No, but it's a good bet,' he finally answered. 'I bought him at the yearling sales this week, on excellent advice, and he has the bloodline and form to win the big race.'

Daisy recovered enough breath to coolly state, 'I

don't gamble.' She lied through her teeth as she added, 'I wish you luck, Mr Cartwright,' then turned her back on him to effect some fast distance from the troublesome encounter.

'All of life is a gamble, Daisy Donahue,' he floated after her.

Not for her it wasn't, and no way was she going to acknowledge the comment by looking back at him.

They all had money to burn, these people. Having worked the past three months with Lynda Twiggley whose PR agency organised events for A-list socialites, Daisy was constantly amazed and scandalised by how much they spent on having a good time. The pre-Christmas parties had been unreal. The New Year's revels, of course, had to be on a luxurious private yacht for the fireworks around Sydney Harbour to be viewed. Now anyone who was anyone was up on Queensland's Gold Coast for the annual Magic Millions carnival—the first big horse-racing event on the calendar.

It had begun earlier this week with the yearling sales, the largest sale of thoroughbreds in Australia. No doubt Ethan Cartwright had paid an enormously extravagant amount for Midas Magic, and had been celebrating his successful bid ever since. There'd been a ball, a swag of cocktail parties, and today was the day to cap it all off, the third richest race day of the year with almost five million dollars in prize money. Daisy sourly hoped his horse would run last.

All of life should not be a gamble.

Some things should be secure.

Like her parents' home.

If helping to make it secure meant staying in this

rotten job, she would grit her teeth and do it, despite the severe heartburn it gave her.

Ethan had not been having a good time. He'd slipped away from the gaggle of women whose frivolous chatter bored him and then been cornered by Lynda Twiggley who was bent on getting him to handle her investments, which was even more boring and distasteful since this carnival was supposed to be fun, not work. The PR specialist had certainly not been using her expertise on him—far too irritatingly pushy—and her manner towards her assistant had bordered on contemptible.

Daisy Donahue…

Now there was a woman who did interest him—the little brown sparrow amongst all the glitzy parrots, playing the meek servant when there wasn't a meek bone in her body. A pocket dynamo, blasting so much hostile energy at him, it had instantly sparked the urge to engage her in battle. Not that he could, given the unfair circumstances of him being a guest and her being a worker under the eyes of her disapproving employer.

I don't gamble…

Containing herself in such a tight mentality, not running any risks whatsoever, probably had her exploding inside. Ethan found himself thinking he would enjoy liberating her, finding out what she would be like if all that burning passion was released. One thing was certain. Daisy Donahue did not have a frivolous personality. And she wasn't boring, either, he added as he suffered Lynda Twiggley claiming his attention again.

'As I was saying before Dee-Dee interrupted…'

Dee-Dee…what a silly name to give to a person who had so much innate dignity! It also showed a lack of respect for her, which had been obvious in how this un-believably arrogant woman had dealt with Daisy. Ethan held the firm belief that everyone deserved to be treated with respect, regardless of their position in life. He wondered why Daisy put up with it, then realised that in these tough economic times, she was not about to risk being out of work.

He gave Lynda Twiggley five more minutes so she wouldn't blame her PA for cutting her business short, then excused himself, saying, 'I already have a very full client list, Lynda, but I'll check if I can fit you in when I get back to my office.' He nodded towards his best friend who was chatting up one of the top-line models. 'Mickey Bourke told me we should talk to the jockey before the big race and it's time I went and collected him.'

'Oh!' Her face fell in disappointment before she summoned up a big parting smile. 'I'll go straight away and place a bet on Midas Magic.'

He didn't care if she did or not. He just wanted to get away from her. Mickey had talked him into this horse business, insisting he needed some outside in-terest to lighten up his life and get him into the social whirl again after his grim disillusionment with his ex-fiancée. A bit of fun, Mickey had argued, especially if Ethan was *off* women.

According to his friend, there was nothing better than the rush of excitement one felt when watching your horse win a big race. Ethan had yet to feel it. Though Mickey should know. His father was one of the most successful thoroughbred trainers in Australia.

Mickey had been born and bred to the horse business. Even at school he would organise sweeps for the

Melbourne Cup—strictly against the rules but he always got away with it. He'd been the livewire in their class—bright, witty, charming—a golden boy with his sun-bleached streaky blond hair and sparkling blue eyes. A natural athlete, too, which was one thing they did have in common, along with their tall, powerful physiques.

Everyone liked Mickey. He was always amusing company. Why he'd chosen to attach himself to Ethan—the quiet, intense student, and his fiercest competitor on the playing fields—had seemed weirdly perverse of him until Mickey had explained.

'No bullshit, okay? I'll give it to you straight. In the quality stakes you're a top-notch contender and I'm naturally drawn to quality. I enjoy the way you think and the way you do things. You could easily cut the rest of us down but you don't. That makes you a great guy in my book.'

The straight face had then broken into a gleeful grin. 'Besides, there are several big advantages in being your friend. First up you're great camouflage. All the schoolmasters think the sun shines out of you, being such a star in class. If I stick with you, the respect they have for you rubs off on me and no one will suspect me of getting up to mischief. Besides which, you're a whiz at numbers and percentages, working out the odds. I like that. I really do respect that. I figure you're going to be a lot of use to me further down the track.'

It was his first demonstration of how smart Mickey was—smart in a way Ethan had not been familiar with, being the only child of dyed-in-the wool academics who did everything by the book, straight down the line. Ethan had instantly decided he could learn a lot from Mickey Bourke who was clearly a very shrewd operator.

'And to me, the writing is already on the wall,' Mickey had continued, adopting a mock-resigned air. 'It's in the way your mind works, Ethan. It homes in on what's absolutely pertinent. You see the play. Your anticipation is incredible. So, regardless of how well I perform on the playing field, I know it will be you the coach will pick to be captain of the cricket team and the rugby. My best choice is to win your friendship, stand at your side and share in your glory.'

Ethan had liked his honesty, his realistic reading of the situation, and his pragmatic judgement of how he could get the most out of his time at school. Other boys might have hated the guy who had the edge on them for the most enviable positions, seen him as the enemy. He and Mickey had ended up the closest of allies in everything, their friendship so solid it had lasted through the years despite their career paths being very different.

They were both still bachelors. 'Too many lovely fish in the sea to settle on one,' was Mickey's attitude. Ethan had long ago reached the cynical conclusion—recently and painfully reinforced by a woman he'd thought was different—that all desirable females had princess personalities, wanting everything their own way and generally bartering sex to get it. Which he'd been reasonably content to go along with. What man didn't want sex?

But every last one of them had been only interested in what he could give them in return for the use of their bodies and the ego trip of being publicly partnered by them. It was an ego trip for the women, too, being seen with him. After all, it was a feather in their cap to have ensnared the interest—however briefly—of one of Sydney's most eligible billionaires.

He would never forget the rotten downer of overhearing Serena preening over her triumphant catch to one of her girlfriends. It would have been a huge mistake to marry her and Ethan hated making mistakes. He still burned over the memory of how deceived he had been in her character.

He wanted honesty in a relationship. He wanted reality. He wanted to be known and appreciated for the person he was. He wanted a woman to give him the kind of understanding companionship that Mickey did. Which was probably impossible because women weren't men. However, if he could just meet one of them who didn't give him the feeling of being buttered up for the kill...

Daisy Donahue slid straight into his mind. It was a pity she wasn't a guest here today. She'd sparked a very lively interest. Not the slightest hint of buttering up from her blunt tongue. The little brown sparrow was full of fireworks which he'd found surprisingly sexy. Nice curvy body, too. He didn't understand Mickey's attraction to models whose stick-like figures had no appeal to him. *They* couldn't swish their non-existent bottoms at him, as Daisy had when she'd made off into the crowd. A very perky bottom.

Booty, the fashionistas called it these days. The word made him smile. He bet Daisy Donohue had *booti-ful* hair, as well, if she ever let it down from the tight knot she'd wound it into at the nape of her neck. Ethan briefly fantasised about letting it down himself, massaging her scalp, getting into her head, watching those blazing dark eyes melt into hot chocolate. He would enjoy that. He really would.

Having reached the edge of the social circle gathered

around Mickey, he caught his friend's eye and nodded towards the exit from the marquee. Not waiting for Mickey to extract himself, Ethan moved on towards it, putting a forbiddingly purposeful expression on his face to discourage anyone from making another unwelcome approach. Mickey caught up with him just as he stepped outside.

'Saw the Twiggley trying to get her claws into you,' he remarked with a sympathetic grin. 'Guess she's one of the wounded, wanting the doctor.'

Ethan grimaced. 'I'm not a doctor.'

'Same thing…fixing up financial fall-out.'

'I prefer the clients who trusted my advice in the first place.'

'Like me.' Mickey clapped him on the shoulder, obviously in high good humour, as they strolled towards the saddling paddock. 'Never doubted your number-crunching for a moment.'

Ethan's mind was still circling around the encounter with Lynda Twiggley. 'She's a revolting woman. Treated her PA like dirt.'

'Hmm…do I detect a note of partiality towards the PA?'

A teasing delight danced in Mickey's blue eyes. He was playing today and he wanted Ethan to play, too. Not that there was any chance of that with Daisy Donahue. Apart from the fact she was unavailable, her hostile glare had hardly been a positive response to him. Though he'd like to tackle the reason for it. Head on. Nothing like a challenge to get the adrenaline running.

'More interesting than your models,' he slung at his friend.

'Ah-ha! This is a good sign that the sly and seductive Serena is no longer casting a pall over your sex drive. So what are you going to do about this new woman of interest?'

'Today she has no time to dally,' he said with a rueful grimace. 'Lynda Twiggley's evil eye is upon her.'

'Easy! Tell the Twiggley you'll take on her financial problems if she releases her PA to you for the rest of the day.'

Giving Daisy no choice? Remembering her stiff-backed pride, Ethan didn't think being traded like a slave would go over too well with her. Besides, he didn't want to work with Lynda Twiggley any more than Daisy did.

'That's not a solution, Mickey. That's a mess,' he mockingly pointed out.

'Well, you figure it out,' he tossed back with a shrug. 'My policy is if you fancy a woman, go after her. Attack the moment. Seize the day. God knows it passes soon enough!'

Ethan rolled his eyes at him. 'Maybe sometimes you should take a longer look before plunging in. As you do with horses.'

Mickey laughed. 'Horses are infinitely more rewarding than women. Forget the PA and concentrate on Midas Magic, Ethan. He'll give you a better run for your money.'

Having moved on to his favourite subject, Mickey regaled Ethan with a potted history of the jockey he was to meet, his many successful rides and his natural empathy with horses—best man for the job today.

Although he listened and made all the expected responses as they strolled on to the saddling paddock, Ethan did not forget Daisy Donahue. She was like a burr in his mind. And his body. He felt a quixotic urge to rescue her from Lynda Twiggley, make whatever was wrong for her right.

Absurd, really.

He knew so little about her.

Yet his instincts kept insisting she might be worth knowing and he could very well regret not pursuing the interest she stirred.

Seize the day…

The big question was…how to do it?

CHAPTER TWO

THE big race gave Daisy the chance to rest for a few minutes. Quite a few guests had left the marquee to watch the horses being led to the starting gates. The rest of them had their attention glued to the television screens. No one was going to make a fuss about anything while their interest was totally captivated by what was happening on the racetrack.

She found a chair and sat down to give her feet a break. The TV commentator was giving a run-down on each yearling—its bloodline, owner, trainer, the colours the jockey was wearing. Gold and black for Midas Magic. Daisy grimaced as she heard that. Of course, the money man would have chosen gold. And he'd be more in the black if the wretched horse won. No depressing red debts for him.

She thought glumly of her parents' situation—ordinary people who'd worked hard to bring up and educate five children and finally believing they could afford the luxury of renovating their home—a new kitchen, a second bathroom, a playroom for the grandchildren and two extra bedrooms so all the family could come and stay, especially for Easter and Christmas and school holidays. They had mortgaged the house to do it, and the bank which had happily lent the money would just as happily sell the property out from under them if the interest on the loan wasn't paid every month.

And no way would they get the full value of the house in a forced sale, given the current slump in the property market. It wouldn't get her parents out of trouble. Besides, it wasn't fair for them to lose their home at this stage of their lives. They deserved a care-free retirement.

Their investment advisor had got it hopelessly wrong. Last year's share market slide had sliced over thirty percent off their superannuation savings. The resulting loss of income was never going to be recovered. Neither was there any hope of the situation improving during this recession.

The rest of the family wasn't in a position to help. Her three older brothers and one sister were all married with young families, struggling to make ends meet. Two of her brothers, Ken and Kevin, had been laid off by their employers in the workforce squeeze. Keith had gone into business for himself and was feeling the pinch. Violet, her sister, had an autistic son who needed so much care, her marriage was very rocky because of it. They simply couldn't cope with more pressure on their shoulders.

Which meant she was the only one who could carry the load. By far the youngest—the late accidental pregnancy—she had moved back to her parents' suburban home in Ryde to give them the rent money she'd been paying for her share-apartment in the inner city, as well as covering most of the food bills to ensure her parents didn't stint on their diet in their anxiety over the debt.

Her contribution meant the monthly interest bill could be paid, but it was an endless cycle. She didn't make enough money to pay off the loan.

What really irked her was if her parents had sought out Ethan Cartwright to manage their nest-egg... But how were ordinary people supposed to know *he* was the man to go to? There'd been no publicity about him until after the economic crash. Besides, he probably only dealt with multi-millionaires. The big spenders in this marquee only mixed with each other.

The commentator's voice rose several decibels as the race began, calling out a string of names. A hubbub of excitement broke out from the spectators gathered in front of the television screens. Daisy rigidly refused to look, resenting how much money these people were prepared to risk on stupid bets. It was a well-known fact that race-fixing went on all the time. If you weren't *in the know*...although perhaps the Magic Millions was different with all the owners wanting their new purchases to perform well in such a prestige event.

'Midas Magic hits the front at the turn and is starting to leave the field behind. He's two lengths ahead... three...four...no one's going to catch him!'

The screaming from the commentator assaulted her ears. And her heart. The man who had everything was about to get a lot more with his horse winning this race. It wasn't fair. It vexed her even further that he'd put her *in the know* and she had ignored his advice, sticking to her principles of not taking any gambles. Besides, who could believe that any horse was a sure thing?

Lynda Twiggley for one!

Daisy scrambled guiltily to her feet as her employer came bursting out of a group of people, gleefully brandishing a betting ticket and catching her PA sitting down on the job. 'I won! I won!' she cried. 'Isn't it marvellous? Ten thousand lovely dollars!'

'Ten thousand?' Daisy repeated, totally stunned by the amount.

'Yes. I wouldn't have taken such a plunge on a horse if Ethan Cartwright hadn't recommended it,' Lynda archly confided. 'Such a gorgeous, clever man! He's made my day!'

'I'm very pleased for you, Miss Twiggley,' Daisy managed to force out. At least it had put her employer in a good mood, unlikely to snipe at any shortcomings she perceived in her PA.

The glittery blue eyes narrowed in determined calculation. 'Now I must get him to look at my shares portfolio. If I can net him into another tête-á-tête, don't interrupt us for anything, Dee-Dee. Should any problem arise, use your own initiative to solve it. That's what I've trained you for.'

'I won't go near him,' Daisy firmly promised.

She couldn't stand seeing him shine with triumph anyway. It would be sickening. Privately she thought her employer had little chance of *netting* him again. Ethan Cartwright had tried to hang onto the diversion of Daisy's gaffe in interrupting their last encounter, insisting on being properly introduced, continuing to speak to her despite Lynda's obvious impatience for her to be gone.

He wouldn't have bothered trying to connect with her under ordinary circumstances. She was way beneath his notice. He'd simply been using her for his own purpose—breaking up a meeting he didn't like. She wished she could dismiss him from her mind. Everything he stood for stirred her up. Worst of all was the fact that she'd felt an undeniable physical attraction to the man. Which was understandable, given that he was a stand-out male, but she hated him all the more for it, making her want what she knew could never be available to her.

'I'd kill for a cup of coffee right now. I wish they'd get on with serving it.'

The whining complaint from one of the models— very much a VIP, having been chosen to star on the runway for Victoria's Secret—sent Daisy straight to the catering tent to investigate the delay. Lynda Twiggley would have a fit if she heard one of her prized guests being put out by any failure in the arrangements made for their pleasure and comfort. Bad PR. It was up to Daisy to prevent or fix anything bad.

Two of the chefs were having a raging argument and their assistants all looked rigid with tension, doing nothing but watching from the sidelines. This catering outfit was being very highly paid to do a top-class job and they weren't delivering. Daisy steeled herself to walk right into the line of fire between the fighting chefs and remind them of their prime responsibility.

'People are asking for coffee,' she stated briskly, giving both of them a stern look. 'It should be out there being served. VIP guests don't like to be left wanting anything.'

It startled them into turning their attention to her.

'It's also supposed to be accompanied by chocolates and petits-fours. Are they ready to go?' she ran on, re-minding them of what was expected, then adding a sensible warning. 'You don't want to lose your good reputation with these people. They always remember delays like this.'

One of the temperamental chefs threw up his hands

and glared around at the motionless staff. 'Move! Move! Get on with it!'

Satisfied she had made her point, Daisy returned to the VIP marquee, intending to assure the model that coffee was on its way. She stopped in her tracks when she saw Ethan Cartwright chatting to her. Venomous thoughts exploded in her head. Nothing but the best for a man like him! She'd known—of course, she'd known—he wasn't really interested in a little brown cow. This was reality—birds of a feather flocked together.

No doubt the magnificent model had taken his advice to bet on Midas Magic, too. The two high-flyers were both beaming with the pleasure of victory, making Daisy's stomach churn from the terrible injustice of it all.

Ethan felt it again, his whole body tingling from a blast of electric energy. He turned his head, his gaze instinctively homing in on the source—Daisy Donahue, her eyes blazing at him with feral animosity, stirring the urge to do battle with her, catch her, cage her until she was tamed to his satisfaction. The weird, exciting thoughts raced through his mind, swiftly followed by Mickey's catch-cry—seize the day.

He'd looked for her without success when he'd re-entered the marquee after the race. Now here she was a few metres away, within easy reach, the challenge she threw out drawing him like a magnet. He automatically started to move towards her, their eyes locked in a duel of sizzling passion.

'Ethan?'

The full-of-herself model he'd been talking to was

calling him back. He'd forgotten his manners. 'Please excuse me, Talia,' he swiftly tossed back at her. 'Someone I have to see.'

In that brief moment of disengagement with Daisy she'd taken flight, dodging behind groups of people, apparently intent on hiding from him. It spurred Ethan on to catch up with her, force a face-to-face confrontation. He sliced through the throng, his interest aroused to an intensity that surprised him, his heart beating like a battle drum as he intercepted her attempted escape, making it impossible for her not to acknowledge him.

'Hello, again,' he said, revelling in the flush of angry frustration that flooded into her cheeks, giving her pale, flawless skin a peaches-and-cream vivacity, making the eyes that warred with his in flaming fury even brighter.

His abrupt appearance in front of her had shocked her into stillness, but it was the stillness of a tightly coiled spring, nerves twanging at the suppression of movement away from him. Her chin jerked up belligerently. The brown pill-box hat slid slightly from its perch on top of her head. He barely restrained himself from reaching up and straightening it for her. He wanted contact—intimate contact—with this woman.

'Mr Cartwright...' she bit out, obviously hating being trapped into this encounter.

He smiled, intent on pouring soothing balm over whatever was making her bristle in his presence. 'Let's make that Ethan.'

She sucked in a quick breath, her eyes flaring a denial of any familiarity between them. 'Congratulations on your win,' she said tersely. 'I didn't place a bet on your horse.

As I told you before, I don't gamble, so there's nothing more to say, is there? We have nothing in common.'

Ethan was not about to let his feet be cut out from under him before he'd even started to make inroads on getting to know her. He turned his smile into an ironic grimace. 'I need some assistance.'

She raised a disbelieving eyebrow, offering him no encouragement to spell it out.

'That is your job, isn't it? Assisting any of the guests here who have a problem?' he pushed.

'What is your problem, Mr Cartwright?' she demanded, her eyes glinting open scepticism.

'You are, Daisy Donahue.'

She frowned, her certainty that he had no problem shifting into a flicker of fear. 'What do you mean?'

'I have the curious sensation that you're shooting mental bullets at me all the time. I'd like you to tell me why.'

For a moment her face went totally blank, as though a switch had been thrown and defensive shutters had instantly clicked into place. He watched her labouring to construct an apologetic expression—a sheer act of will, against her natural grain. Her eyes took on a pleading look, begging his forgiveness. Her mouth softened into an appealing little smile. She spoke in a tone that mocked herself.

'I've just had to deal with some trouble in the catering tent and it may cause more trouble. I'm sorry if I've channelled my own angst onto you, Mr Cartwright. I didn't mean to attract your attention. In fact, you'll be doing me a great favour if you'll walk away from me right now. My boss won't like it if she sees you talking to me.'

'Surely as a guest I'm entitled to speak to whomever I like,' he argued.

'I'm not a guest and I'm taking up your time—time Miss Twiggley would prefer you to spend with her,' she said pointedly.

'I've said all I intend to say to Lynda Twiggley.'

'That's not my business. If I don't stay clear of you, my job might very well be at risk. So please excuse me, Mr Cartwright.'

'Be damned if I will!' Frustration fumed through him. His hand snaked out and grabbed her arm as she turned away to escape him again. 'This isn't the Dark Ages!' he shot out before she could voice a protest.

'Oh, yes, it is!' she retorted with blistering scorn, the defence system cracking wide open at being forcibly held. Wild hostility poured into wild accusation. 'You're acting like a feudal lord manhandling a servant girl who can't fight back.'

The image was wrong. She could fight back. She was doing it with all her mental might. But for once in his life Ethan wanted to be a feudal lord, having his way with this woman. He knew he should release her yet his mind had lost all sense of civilised behaviour. Imposing this physical link with her was arousing a host of primitive feelings that demanded satisfaction.

'You're denying me the assistance I asked for,' he argued.

'With good reason,' she hotly returned.

'Nonsense! It's totally unreasonable!'

'What is the matter with you?' she cried in exasperation. 'Why bother with me when—?'

'Because you bother me more than anyone here.'

'What? Because I'm not seeking your attention? Are

you so used to women hanging on your every word, your high and mighty ego is pricked by one who doesn't?'

'You did want my attention, Daisy Donahue,' he slung back at her in burning certainty. 'You were looking at me.'

She tried to explain it away, biting out the words with icy precision. 'The model you were talking to had complained about coffee not having been served. I had intended to inform her it was on its way when I saw you with her.' Her teeth were bared in a savagely mocking smile. 'Mindful of my boss's instructions and contrary to your arrogant assumption, I didn't want to draw any more attention from you, Mr Cartwright.'

Ethan was not convinced. It wasn't dismissal he'd felt coming from her. It had been a powerful bolt of passion aimed directly at him. It was still hitting him. His whole body was energised by it. His eyes derided her evasion of the truth as he attacked her reading of his character.

'You can stick me with ego and arrogance as much as you like, but there's more going on in your head than you're telling me, and it has nothing to do with Lynda Twiggley's instructions.'

'What I think is my business,' she whipped back.

'Not when it involves me.'

Impasse.

She glared at him, the wheels of her mind going round and round in a fierce search for an exit line he might accept.

He wanted to drag her into his embrace and kiss her until all her resistance melted. Never had he been so aroused by a woman. For the first time in his life he was in total tune with the cavemen of old who simply hauled off the object of their desire and took their pleasure at will. Was it her hostility that excited him? Had he grown too bored with women who were only too eager in their compliance?

Intensity…the word leapt into his mind. That was what had been lacking in all his other connections with women. Daisy Donahue was transmitting it, hitting the same chord in him. Normally he channelled it into his work. It wasn't a social asset. Intensity disturbed people. Too dark, Mickey said. But there was a dark side to Daisy Donahue, too, setting off a weird wave of exhilaration through his bloodstream. And a compulsion to explore it.

She dragged in a deep breath and tore her gaze from his, dropping it pointedly to the hand still grasping her arm. He softened his grip, rubbing his thumb along the underside of her wrist, finding the beat of her pulse, exulting in its rapid drumming.

She was excited, too.

Or was it fear?

'I'm sorry I bothered you, Mr Cartwright,' she said in a stilted little voice. Her beautifully feminine breasts lifted as she filled her lungs again. Her eyes met his in a plea that held a vulnerability he hadn't seen before in her. 'Please let me go.'

It made him feel like a cad for holding her against her will, yet he couldn't bring himself to let her go. 'You said we have nothing in common. I think we do, Daisy Donahue.'

She shook her head, agitation flickering into definite fear as she was distracted by something behind him.

'Ah, Dee-Dee,' came the smarmy voice of Lynda Twiggley who was obviously about to insinuate herself into the situation.

'Miss Twiggley,' she said in a shaky subservient tone as the woman stepped forward to part them.

It enfuriated Ethan that Daisy should feel it necessary to kowtow to her snaky employer. She was a natural-born fighter. It was wrong for her to be in this position.

'Catering needs a prompt to get the coffee moving.'

It was a dismissive command.

Daisy tried to pull her arm free, anxious to avoid any more displeasure being heaped on her head.

Ethan tightened his grip, determined on keeping her with him.

'Daisy has already done that,' he coldly told the Twiggley who turned an ingratiating smile to him.

'Then she can do it again,' was the unbending reply.

Unreasonable, demanding bitch!

Ethan lost his cool. 'Miss Twiggley…' grated out from between gnashing teeth.

She fluttered her exquisitely painted fingernails and her false eyelashes at him. 'Oh, do make it Lynda, please…'

It revolted him. Words shot out of his mouth in a stream of searing contempt without any thought to their consequences.

'I think it's time you stopped treating your PA like a slave who doesn't warrant any consideration or courtesy.'

Her mouth gaped open in shock.

He felt a shudder run up Daisy's arm.

The ensuing silence was impregnated with the hair-prickling sense that a bomb had just gone off. Ethan revelled in its intensity. He was so off his coolly analytical brain—no number-crunching going on at all—he was actually looking forward to the fall-out.

CHAPTER THREE

DAISY'S mind was reeling. Her heart was galloping faster than any racehorse. Any second now her boss was going to throw a major tantrum and she'd bear the brunt of it. Ethan Cartwright was too important a person to cop the whiplash from his strike on her behalf.

Why had he done it?

Why, why, why…?

Even if he'd meant well, he should have known it would rebound on her. He just hadn't cared. It wasn't going to affect his life. He was an untouchable. Anger at not getting his own way with her had spilled over onto Lynda Twiggley. Never mind that Daisy was the one who would pay for it—the selfish, arrogant pig! She'd explained the situation to him, begged him to let her go, and what he'd done was put her job at risk—the job she had to keep or see her parents' home go down the bankruptcy drain.

Panic ripped through her stomach as her boss started puffing herself up to let fly her ferocious temper. Mean blue eyes cut her to ribbons. The attack had the cyclonic force of a fireball.

'How dare you complain about how I treat you, you ungrateful little cow!'

'I didn't! I swear I didn't!' Daisy babbled.

'I speak from my own observation,' Ethan Cartwright sliced in.

It didn't improve the situation. It made it a thousand times worse. Being subjected to such personal criticism from him was so offensive, Lynda turned to him in a towering rage, probably thinking her bid to have him fix her financial affairs had been sabotaged and Daisy knew she was going to be blamed for it, regardless of anything Ethan Cartwright said.

'I pay her very well to do what I tell her. There's nothing slavish about that, I assure you,' she hissed at him, steam pouring from her.

'I take exception to you telling her to stay away from me,' he shot back. 'That's not work. It's—'

Lynda exploded into a tirade at Daisy, cutting Ethan Cartwright off in mid-speech. 'You stupid, stupid girl! Have you no sense of discretion, no brain in your head? Might I remind you that you signed a confidentiality clause in your contract with me. Which you've just broken in the worst possible way with your stupid, wagging tongue.'

She *had* committed the indiscretion.

It was impossible to defend herself.

What could she say…that Ethan Cartwright's persistence had goaded her into it? No way would that be an acceptable excuse. She had not put her boss's interests first. The chaotic effect he had on her had overwhelmed her usual grasp of what was permissible.

Daisy stood in appalled silence, quaking inside as the storm broke over her, her heart sinking as she realised there was no hope of this being forgiven or forgotten.

The inevitable lightning struck.

'You're fired! As of now!'

She felt the blood draining from her face.

The thunder rolled on. 'And don't come back to the office. I'll have your personal things parcelled up and sent home. Untrustworthy blabbermouth!'

Lynda Twiggley's last look of furious disgust barely penetrated the dizziness flooding through Daisy's head. Like some fade-out on a television screen, the back of her ex-employer disintegrated into dots.

Ethan caught her as she started to fall, scooping her into a tight embrace. It was where he'd wanted Daisy Donahue but not limp and unconscious. He had to get her firing on all cylinders again. With a quick stoop to hook an arm under her knees, he lifted her off her feet, cradling her across his chest.

A chair was needed—set her down, lower her head to get some blood back in it, a glass of water…that was what common sense said, yet as he started carrying her towards one, he was riven by the strong temptation to keep right on going, out of the marquee, into a limousine and off to his cave. He'd caught his woman. She felt good in his arms. He wanted her out of this jungle of people and completely to himself.

Problem was she'd probably come to before he got her to the limousine. How long did a faint last? And she'd undoubtedly throw a scene at the hotel before he could take her to his suite.

No, it was a mad idea.

A sheikh might get away with it.

Or a buccaneer of old who was captain of his own ship.

Not Ethan Cartwright in this modern world of political correctness. *He* would have to answer for his actions.

Nevertheless, he was almost at the exit to the marquee when Mickey caught up with him. 'Hey, Ethan. You doing a runner with the girl?'

It stopped him. He turned to his friend whose face was alight with fascinated curiosity. 'She fainted. I have to get her to a chair.'

'You've passed a whole bunch of them.'

'Distracted,' Ethan muttered. He hadn't been aware of anything except the woman in his arms—the feelings she generated in him.

'Over here,' Mickey directed, steering him towards one as Daisy stirred in his arms, her lovely full breasts swelling against the wall of his chest as she gulped in air.

Ethan told himself his brain needed a blast of oxygen, too. As much as he wanted to hang onto Daisy Donahue she was going to rip into him the moment she had regained her wits. He'd be enemy number one for causing her to lose her job, regardless of whether or not it had been a good position for a person like her to have. And freeing her from it so she could be with him was not an argument she was about to appreciate. Somehow he would have to make her see him as her saviour instead of the black dog of disaster.

Daisy struggled to regain her strength and her wits. Never in her whole life had she fainted and to have Ethan Cartwright take advantage of this momentary weakness, manhandling her even more than before, was the absolute pits. At least she wasn't being carried by him any more. He'd put her on a chair and was sitting beside her. Despite the fact that he'd shoved her head down to her knees, it was still swimming, and he had his arm around her in support, which she probably needed, though she hated needing anything from him. He'd just destroyed the lifeline to keeping her parents in their home.

'Fetch her a glass of water, will you, Mickey?'

His voice upset her even further, loaded with concern. *After* the event. No concern when it really mattered.

'Sure. And here's her hat. It dropped off on the way.'

Total indignity on top of everything else!

By the time the glass of water came, she was steady enough to lift her head and sip it. 'Thanks,' she muttered to the man who'd brought it—Mickey Bourke, another A-list bachelor with no worries about where his next dollar was coming from.

'I'll look after her now,' Ethan Cartwright said, dismissing his friend.

'Right!' Mickey Bourke grinned at him. 'Nothing like seizing the day! Go for it, man!'

Seizing the day? The phrase scraped over all the jagged edges in Daisy's mind. Her day, her job, a secure future for her parents had all been wrecked by Ethan Cartwright going for what he wanted. She felt like throwing the glass of water in his face, sober up some of the blind ego that had completely overlooked what he'd been doing to her. But what good would that achieve?

Despair squeezed her heart.

'Are you feeling better, Daisy?' he asked caringly.

Nothing could make her feel better. 'Well enough for you to remove your arm,' she answered tersely, sitting up straight and stiffening her shoulders to show him his support was no longer needed. Or welcome.

'Okay, but you should keep sitting for a while. Maybe you should eat something. Did you have any lunch?'

No, she hadn't, which might have contributed to her fainting, although she was used to running on empty in this job. Except she didn't have a job any more. Which was all *his fault*.

She turned to face him, anger spurting off her tongue. 'It's a bit late to start caring about me, Mr Cartwright. The damage is done.'

He grimaced, but there was no regret in the green eyes boring into hers. 'Lynda Twiggley was doing you a damage, making you bow to her tyranny.'

'I could manage that. If you hadn't interfered, I'd still have my job.'

'You didn't like it,' he said with certainty.

'What's *like* got to do with it?' she cried in exasperation. 'It was the best paid job I've ever had and I need the money. You have no idea how much I need it. You've probably never known a moment's worry over money in your entire life.'

His mouth tilted into an ironic smile. 'Actually I carry the burden of worrying about money all the time.'

'Big money!' she corrected savagely. 'Not life-destroying lack of income.'

He frowned. 'Surely it's not that bad!'

'It most certainly is!' She quickly sipped some more water. The vehement bursts of emotion were making her feel light-headed again. Or maybe it was him sitting so close to her, exerting his mega-male attraction. A woman could drown in those green eyes.

'I'm sorry. I thought you'd be better off in another job,' he said with the first hint of apology.

'You didn't think at all,' she muttered furiously. 'Not on my level.'

'What do you mean…your level?'

She lashed him with grim realities. 'The level where people struggle to make ends meet. Where the job market is getting tighter every day. Where being out of work can bring everything crashing down.'

'Are you in debt?' he asked, his eyes seriously probing hers, making her heart jiggle with the wish he really did care. This was a man who could turn everything around for her parents if he wanted to. And he had a physical magnetism that was getting to her again.

'No. Yes.' She heaved a desolate sigh. 'My parents are. And if I don't pay the interest to the bank, they'll lose their home. They can't do it. It's up to me.'

'Well, there's a twist,' he dryly commented. 'I thought the Y generation lived off their parents, not the other way around.'

He wasn't interested. She'd been stupid to entertain the wild thought, even for a second, that such a high-flyer would come to the rescue of ordinary people.

'You live on a different planet, Ethan Cartwright,' she retorted bitterly.

'I believe in people being responsible for themselves. If your parents incurred a debt, it's up to them to—'

'You don't know anything,' she snapped. 'Sometimes people can't manage for themselves.'

'Okay. Tell me the circumstances,' he invited.

'As if you care!' Her eyes savaged him for his irresponsibility. 'You didn't care about the consequences to me when you ignored my plea to let me go. You didn't care about offending my boss so deeply I didn't have a chance of hanging onto my job. And just how do you think I'm going to get another highly paid position without a glowing reference from Lynda Twiggley? I'm dead in the water.'

She banged her glass down on the floor, stood up, and snatched her hat from his hands. 'Goodbye, Mr Cartwright. I can't say it was pleasure meeting you.'

'Wait!'

He was on his feet so fast and blocking the direct route to the exit of the marquee, Daisy had no choice but to halt and face him again. She lifted a belligerent chin as she demanded, 'What for?'

Ethan didn't have a ready answer. He was acting purely on the need to keep Daisy Donahue in his life. She was magnificent—cheeks flaring with colour again, big brown eyes flashing a fierce challenge at him, her petite figure powering up to fight him. He remembered how her soft, feminine curves had felt when he had been carrying her. Add the vitality of the passion he felt coming from her now…the thought of having all that locked in his arms sent fiery tingles to his groin.

An answer came to him.

He'd created the situation which was driving her away from him.

He had to reverse it.

'I'll give you a job,' he said.

Her eyes widened in astonishment, then narrowed with suspicion. 'What as? Your cleaning lady?'

There was a huge appeal in that image—Daisy on her hands and knees, scrubbing his floors, her perky bottom swaying with the action. But he knew he was dead if he suggested it. His mind whizzed to other possibilities. He didn't need a PA. His business was fully staffed. No room for her there. So what could he offer that she wouldn't turn down flat?

'You need a lifeline, right?' he said, hedging for time to come up with an acceptable rescue package. 'A stopgap until you can find a job that suits you?'

'If I have to clean floors, I will, but they won't be yours,' she vowed rebelliously, one hip jutting out as she stuck a hand on it, emphasising the fascinating smallness of her waist. 'You are the last person I want to do anything for right now.'

Ethan smothered a sigh. Feudal lord and serving girl was not an appealing picture to her. Although if he wrapped it up in gold paper...

'How about executive housekeeper? I've recently bought a property I've started on renovating. You could oversee the tradesmen's work, ensure that everything's kept in order. I'll pay you the same salary you earned with Lynda Twiggley.'

The fight in her eyes wavered into a sea of vulnerable uncertainty—the need for no break in her money chain warring with a mountain of doubts about what she might be getting into by putting herself in his power. Her throat moved convulsively. She was swallowing hard. And blinking hard.

'Are you serious?' she asked huskily.

'Yes. I'm sorry for causing you so much distress,' he said quietly, realising she was desperately trying to stem a gush of tears. 'The least I can do is tide you over until you find better ground for yourself.'

She bit her lips. Her eyelashes swept down. She lowered her head. Her hand dropped from her hip and fretted at the pill-box hat she was holding in her other hand. 'It might be months before I can find another job,' she mumbled anxiously.

'I expect the renovations will go on for months. It's a messy business. It will be good to have someone on site, checking up on everything. Even the most reputable builders need a critical eye on them to get it all right and clean up after themselves. In effect, you'd be my PA for a special project. Okay?'

The eyelashes slowly fluttered up again. He had the weird sense of his heart turning over as she looked earnestly at him. 'You're really serious about this? You'll pay me as much as Lynda Twiggley did?'

Down to the bartering line again, he thought with his usual cynicism, but if that's what it took to get this woman he'd do it. He reached for his wallet. 'I'll give you an advance on your salary to seal the deal.'

She stared at his bulging wallet as he opened it—the hook that never failed to work.

'How much were you being paid? A couple of thousand a week?' He riffled through the notes, prepared to give her any sum she nominated. It was irrelevant to him. He'd just won two million dollars in prize money on Midas Magic.

She shook her head.

'More? Less?' he prompted.

Her gaze lifted, meeting his with steely pride. 'I don't take money I haven't earned, Mr Cartwright. My salary was fifteen hundred dollars a week before tax. If you're satisfied with what I can do for you after the first week of being your on-site PA, I'd appreciate it if you'd pay me then.'

'Fine!' he agreed, barely hiding the jolt of surprise at her refusal to grab the money.

Honesty…fair play…Daisy Donahue was exhibiting a fine sense of both, making him feel slightly uncomfortable about having his own secret agenda.

'Where is this property?' she asked.

'Hunters Hill.'

She pressed him for more details, weighing up the information he gave, assuring herself there was a genuine job to be done. Once they'd settled on a meeting at the house at eight o'clock on Monday morning of the next week, she took her leave of him, very firmly, and Ethan let her go, watching the seductive swish of her bottom, content with the thought he'd be seeing a lot more of Daisy Donahue in the very near future.

He was looking forward to it.

In fact, he couldn't remember looking forward to a meeting with a woman quite so much!

CHAPTER FOUR

HUNTERS HILL...*the* wealthiest suburb in Sydney, according to one of the Sunday newspapers. Daisy also recalled reading that a famous Australian actress had a home there, along with other celebrities. It was no surprise that Ethan Cartwright had chosen to buy a property in such a prestigious area. Birds of a feather definitely flocked together.

Why he had chosen to pursue some kind of acquaintance with her at the Magic Millions race-day was odd in the extreme. She could only think his ego had been piqued by her dismissive behaviour. They had nothing in common. Absolutely nothing. Except they were both now paying for the outcome of that encounter—he offering her a job out of guilt, she taking it because there was no other choice immediately available.

It was far from an ideal situation, and as she drove her little car towards the address he had given, she felt increasingly anxious about whether there would be anything of real value she could do for what he would be paying her. Builders were messy and often careless. She knew that from when her parents had renovated their home. Nevertheless, she suspected that for much of the time she'd simply be watching and twiddling her thumbs.

Fortunately Hunters Hill was not a long or difficult trip from her parents' home in Ryde, much less hassle than going across the Harbour Bridge to Lynda Twiggley's office at Woolloomooloo. At least she would save on petrol while she worked for Ethan Cartwright. Her Hyundai Getz was a very economical car, but the price of fuel still hurt.

Anxious not to be late, Daisy had given herself plenty of time to arrive at her destination before eight o'clock. The nearer she got to it, the more impressive the properties became—big old homes set in much larger grounds than any normal suburban block. Some were massive and built of sandstone which would be horrendously expensive these days, but this was an old established area in Sydney, close to the harbour and at the mouth of the Lane Cove River.

She couldn't imagine Ethan Cartwright living in any of them. Why would a bachelor want to rattle around alone in a mansion when a luxurious apartment right in the CBD would provide an easier lifestyle? No doubt he had simply made a shrewd investment. Even the top end of the property market had slumped—dropping millions of dollars in recent months—so it was an opportune time to buy. It was the best time to renovate, too, with so many builders out of work. He'd probably bought an old home in bad repair but on prime real estate, and was anticipating making a huge profit when fortunes changed again.

There were several tradesmen's trucks parked along the designated street when Daisy turned into it, more or less marking the place she had to find. Confirmation of the address brought a flood of amazement. It *was* a mansion and it looked absolutely beautiful the way it was, at least on the outside.

The huge, white, two-storeyed house had been built with perfect symmetry, the windows and doors—all of which had French doors that opened out—matching up on both floors, which also had perfectly matching verandahs with glorious white wrought-iron railings. The roof was dark grey slate and a wide set of bluestone steps led up from a semi-circular driveway to the front door. Within this semi-circle was a large stone fountain.

There were no gardens, just green lawn and trees along the side fence-line, giving the setting a wonderful simplicity that highlighted the splendid grace of the house. The front fence and two side double gates were also of white wrought-iron in the same pattern as the verandah railings. One set of gates was open, obviously for the workmen's use, as there was another driveway down that side of the house to the back.

A black BMW roadster was parked at the foot of the front steps—definitely a billionaire's car, which meant her new employer was already here waiting for her. Daisy decided to drive into the grounds and park behind it. After all, she was supposed to be in charge of this project, right on site.

If Ethan Cartwright hadn't changed his mind in the meantime.

It was a worry.

Her parents had both been very dubious about what they saw as an impulsive and irregular offer of work Daisy wasn't trained for. She'd had to explain the circumstances of losing her job to them and they were only too painfully aware of why she had accepted this one. Her father kept muttering, 'It isn't right,' and they should sell up and move somewhere cheaper—a place in one of the housing estates for senior citizens.

Daisy couldn't bear the thought of that happening. Not only did it deeply wound her sense of justice, but it would also completely change the dynamics of the family. She'd insisted this was only a stopgap solution until she found another proper job and they weren't to worry. She was perfectly capable of managing anything she set her mind to.

Nevertheless, her confidence wasn't so easy to hang onto as she alighted from her car and started up the steps. Her stomach felt downright jittery. She told herself it was caused more by the prospect of having to meet Ethan Cartwright again—being subjected to his powerfully male charisma and those riveting green eyes—than trying to keep a check on the work of a team of tradesmen. Once *he* was gone and out of her hair, she'd be fine.

Not that he'd been in her hair. Neither was she about to let him anywhere near it. The tug of his sheer sexual impact on her female hormones was warning enough that she was dangerously attracted to the man, despite the huge differences between them. She had to maintain a hands-off policy whenever he plagued her with his presence. The way his touch affected her was far too disturbing. It could draw her into very foolish behaviour.

Today she had deliberately chosen a very downmarket appearance—a loose cotton tunic printed with daisies on a blue background, blue jeans, flat sneakers on her feet making her look even smaller in stature, a blue scrunchy holding her long, brown hair back in a ponytail, and no make-up apart from pink-brown lipstick, which was next to nothing.

It had to be patently clear to him that she was not

aiming to be an object of desire in his eyes. Though she couldn't really imagine she ever had been anyway. His pursuit of her on the Magic Millions race-day had definitely been an ego thing, not an attraction thing, and this whole business now was a fix-up thing, which was purely temporary. The X-factor problem was all on her side and it had to be kept hidden.

Having reached the front door, she took a deep, calming breath and pressed the call button. Ethan Cartwright did not give her time to twiddle her thumbs. The door was opened within seconds and the oxygen Daisy had drawn in was instantly trapped in her lungs.

The man was utterly, utterly gorgeous.

He was dressed in a superbly tailored dark grey suit, white shirt and a silk tie striped in red, grey and green. Some nose-prickling exotic cologne had been splashed on his strong, freshly shaven jaw. His thick, black hair flopped onto his forehead in an endearing wave. The green eyes sparkled as though he was delighted to see her and his smile kicked her heart into thumping like a drum.

'Good morning!' he said cheerfully, his rich male voice making her ears tingle.

'Hi!' was all she managed to croak.

'Come on in and I'll show you around,' he invited, stepping back and waving her forward.

He's not for me, he's not for me, he's not for me, her mind wildly recited as she willed her feet to move. The job was obviously still on. All she had to do was be sensible and adopt a strictly practical attitude.

The verandah had been tiled in a grey-and-white diamond pattern. This was repeated in the wide hallway she stepped into, but with an inset border featuring a black-and-white scroll. This border led to and framed a central staircase which curved up to the top floor, the balustrade painted in a shiny black lacquer, the steps carpeted in dark red.

'Wow!' she murmured.

'Do you like the red?' he asked, looking quizzically at her.

'Well, the effect is very dramatic,' she said cautiously, unsure if this was some kind of test.

'I'm thinking of recarpeting in green.'

'Green would look good.'

'You don't have to agree,' he said dryly.

'No, I think green would be easier to live with. The red is a bit in your face. Though it's all a matter of taste, isn't it? I wouldn't bother changing it if you're planning to sell. Let the new owner choose.'

'I'm not planning to sell.'

She looked at him in surprise.

His eyes bored in hers. 'I intend to make this *my* place.'

'It's a big place for one person,' she couldn't help commenting.

'I'm tired of living in an apartment. I want space.'

'Well, you've certainly got it here,' she said, barely stopping herself from rolling her eyes at the sheer extravagance of how much space he'd bought for himself.

His mouth quirked. 'You don't think I'll use it all?'

Caution held her tongue again. 'It's not for me to say.'

Amusement danced in his eyes. He ushered her to double doors to the right of the staircase. 'This was the drawing room. It will become my games room.'

'Games?' she queried, looking at the huge expanse

of dark red carpet and the magnificent white fireplace on the far wall, in her mind's eye seeing it furnished in the kind of graceful antiques people put in grand houses.

'All sorts of board games, card games. I have a group of friends who get together to play on Tuesday nights. I've acquired a large collection of games over the years and I'm having shelves and cupboards built along the internal walls in here to house them.'

She shook her head, amazed that a man like him enjoyed such ordinary pastimes. It was what her family did when they got together, playing games around the kitchen table.

'You don't like the idea?' he probed.

'If no expense is to be spared on these renovations, I'd put in a bar as well,' she suggested, a teasing grin breaking out on her face. 'Gaming is thirsty work.'

It was his turn to look surprised. 'You play, too?'

'I'm the current family champion at Scrabble,' she proudly declared. 'And I've been known to clean them all up at poker.'

He laughed, and suddenly there was a connection sizzling between them that knocked every bit of common sense out of Daisy's head. He didn't seem quite so high and mighty, more human like her, and she wished she could join his gaming group on Tuesday nights.

He cocked his head assessingly. 'I hadn't thought of a bar in here, but it would be handy. And a pantry for nibbles. Speak to Charlie about it.'

'Who's Charlie?'

'Charlie Hollier, my architect. He'll be dropping by some time today. Tell him to add a bar and pantry to the plan for this room. It will save trips to the kitchen.'

Just like that, Daisy thought, remembering how obscenely wealthy he was and telling herself that he and his friends undoubtedly played high-stakes poker which she could never afford. Her family counted their wins in plastic chips, no money involved at all.

'Now across the hall…' he led the way, throwing open another set of double doors '…is what used to be the ballroom.'

Daisy goggled at the incredibly splendid, many-tiered, crystal chandelier centred in the high ceiling above a massive room which obviously ran the whole length of the house.

'That's coming down today,' Ethan informed her.

Daisy goggled at him. 'You're getting rid of it?'

'I'm selling it. It's far too valuable to toss out. I was told it was bought from the Paris Exhibition in 1879. Some specialist lighting people will remove it and I'd appreciate it if you ensure they have adequate covering on the floor when they take it down. I don't want the polished floorboards damaged.'

'No, of course not,' she murmured, staring at the floor which gleamed invitingly for dancing feet. 'You don't intend to hold balls in here?'

He laughed. 'I think that era is well and truly gone, Daisy. I'll be putting a billiard table in this top half of the room with appropriate lighting above it. The bottom half of the room will become a home theatre—television, sound system, comfortable lounges.'

She sighed over the loss of the room's original function. 'It seems a shame. Though you're right about more modern living. I guess the floor will still be used for dancing when you throw parties.'

'Mmmh…you like dancing?'

'I *love* dancing. My favourite show on television is one that features up-and-coming dancers competing against each other. It must have been marvellous, waltzing in here.'

The green eyes twinkled wicked temptation. 'I could waltz you around now before the chandelier goes. You could close your eyes and pretend you're back in Victorian times.'

Her blood instantly heated at the idea of him taking her into his arms, pressing her close to him, their thighs brushing seductively as he twirled her across the floor. This terrible attraction to Ethan Cartwright had to be stamped out, not fed. She'd been running off at the mouth instead of simply taking in instructions. That had to stop. She had to keep in her place and he had to keep in his or this job would go haywire before it had even started.

Ignoring the flush on her cheeks, she gave him a stern look designed to banish any dangerous familiarity springing up between them. 'I don't believe the master of the house ever danced with his staff,' she stated emphatically. 'And I think that's a very good principle in general,' she added for good measure.

Ethan couldn't help grinning. Daisy Donahue was priceless. Here she was drawing battle lines, warning him they weren't to be crossed, establishing herself as forbidden territory, shooting the heady spice of challenge straight into his brain. The anticipation that had been bubbling through him as he'd waited for her to arrive this morning was certainly not fizzling out. His delight in her kept escalating. Winning her over to what he wanted was going to be a glorious game.

'I don't think I'll feel like master of the house until all the reconstruction is done,' he said in mock seriousness, his mouth still twitching with a dancing inner joy as he gestured for her to continue accompanying him on a tour of the property.

He felt no prick of conscience about taking advantage of the fact she was working for him. This was a stopgap position for her, not a serious career where business should not be mixed with pleasure. He dismissed that hurdle as of no account whatsoever, and she would surely come to realise that, too. This was a time-out situation—him from his normal social life, which had been soured by Serena, Daisy from the pressure of keeping a job she must have hated. He saw no reason why they shouldn't enjoy the experience of each other, once he'd opened up the desire for it on her side.

They walked down the ballroom and turned into the area which had been remodelled into a modern kitchen and dining area, facing a lovely view of the harbour. 'I designed the kitchen myself and had it put in first so I could move in here,' he told her.

She gave him a startled look. 'You're living here already?'

'Yes. I can't be here during the day but I wanted to check daily progress.'

She heaved a sigh, her gaze fluttering nervously away from his as she muttered, 'Then I'll be seeing you every morning.'

It was a dead giveaway that his presence disturbed her. Ethan was certain that she was as sexually aware of him as he was of her. Why she felt she had to put barriers between them was a mystery, but he was confident of bringing them down sooner or later.

Either curiosity or unease drove her to check out the design of his kitchen, putting some physical distance between them as she busily opened cupboards and looked at everything. Ethan simply enjoyed watching her. She was not a little brown sparrow this morning, more like a fresh flower with the daisy print tunic and her hair pulled up in a pert ponytail. The tight blue jeans did splendid justice to her very cute and sexy derrière.

He wondered how old she was. Today she could pass as a teenager, but the mature experience in her eyes suggested late twenties. He needed to know more about her life. Clearly she had a close involvement with her family, but what about other relationships? Was there a man causing her hands-off attitude towards him—someone she cared about?

Ethan didn't like that idea. He wanted to know and have this woman. Maybe it was the extreme contrast to Serena that struck deep chords in him, the contrast to all the simpering socialites who sought his attention. He felt newly invigorated with Daisy Donahue and he was in absolutely no doubt he sparked some very lively feelings in her, too.

So if the connection went both ways—which it surely did—she couldn't be strongly attached to someone else. Possibly she was struggling with the newness of the whole situation between them, not wanting to risk losing this job. Whatever…he had to persuade her to stop fighting it, go with it, see how far it went, how good it might be. She was so excitingly different from the women he'd known, he was determined on exploring the difference.

'This kitchen would meet the needs of a master chef,' she remarked in some awe.

He smiled. 'I enjoy cooking.'

Her big brown eyes widened in surprise. 'You do?'

'It's relaxing, as well as being a very sensual pleasure.'

He deliberately delivered those words in a provocative drawl, revelling in the betraying heat that coloured her cheeks again.

'A man of many talents,' she said ironically, then with a brisk air strode out from behind the island bench and waved him to show her more. 'What else do I need to see before you leave for work?'

She wanted him gone.

But Daisy Donahue would have to face him—deal with him—day after day.

Ethan was content with that situation.

No matter what she did, the attraction would not go away.

It would keep simmering until flashpoint was reached.

He pointed to the room beyond the dining area. 'That will be my home office. I've left a set of Charlie's plans for all the renovations on the desk in there so you can see what is to be done. Also house keys so you can let yourself in and lock up before you leave. The utility room is between the office and the games room. A powder room is located under the staircase. Bedrooms, dressing rooms and bathrooms are upstairs. You can check them out at your leisure. The major work at the moment is being done outside.'

The next half an hour was spent escorting her around the grounds where a swimming pool was replacing the croquet lawn and the old lawn tennis court on the lower terrace was being given an all-weather surface which didn't require constant maintenance. The old carriage house on one side of the pool area was being updated to a double garage with a storeroom at the back of it, and what used to be the staff quarters on the other side was being transformed into a pool cabana/guest apartment with a barbecue area. He introduced Daisy to all the tradesmen as the on-site manager, giving her the authority to make decisions or refer them to him.

'As you can see, there's a lot going on. Should keep you occupied for months,' he remarked with considerable satisfaction as they strolled back to the house. 'It will be good having you here, overseeing the work.'

She frowned. 'Shouldn't your architect be supervising all this?'

'Oh, Charlie pops in when he can. He does have other projects on the go and can't give this place his exclusive attention. But grill him on anything you feel you need to know when he visits this morning. Okay?'

'Okay.' She slanted him a measuring look. 'You're trusting me with a big responsibility and you hardly know me.'

'You're the responsible type. I have no doubt you're up to the job,' he blithely replied.

The look became more probing. 'What makes you think I'm the responsible type?'

'I observed you working for Lynda Twiggley, taking responsibility to a slavish degree.'

She grimaced. 'I shouldn't have been indiscreet.'

'My fault. I drove you to it. Apart from that, you've taken on the responsibility of servicing your parents' debt,' he reminded her admiringly. 'That tells me you can be counted on to rise to any crisis and deal with it as best you can.'

'Oh!'

The enchanting flush rose in her cheeks again. He couldn't resist brushing the soft warm skin with his fingertips, pretending it was a farewell gesture and a salute of respect. 'Got to go. You'll be fine, Daisy. Don't worry. Just do what you think should be done.'

He took his leave before he was tempted into some extreme indiscretion himself. Slowly, slowly, was the best plan of action with Daisy Donahue, he told himself as he climbed into his BMW. But he couldn't stop himself from driving off with an exhilarating burst of speed.

She was in his house.

Within reach.

Whenever he chose to push the connection.

Maybe she would disappoint him in the end, turn into another princess once she gave in to what he wanted, capitalising on the sexual power a woman could always wield. Whether she did or not was irrelevant right now. She was throwing out a challenge which was totally irresistible and Ethan was not about to be deterred from winning it.

CHAPTER FIVE

DAISY watched Ethan Cartwright drive away with very mixed feelings. Not only was he a sexy devil, she was actually beginning to like him, which was even more unsettling. This situation would be much easier if she could hang onto her former judgement that he was a spoilt, self-centred, arrogant egomaniac who had so much obscene wealth he didn't know or care how ordinary people lived.

All of which was probably still true. It shouldn't make any difference that he was into games and liked doing his own cooking and seemed to admire her for coping with her parents' financial difficulties. *Unlike* her ex-boyfriend who'd thought she was completely off her brain for giving up the city lifestyle that matched his and moving out to Ryde which was totally inconvenient for dating.

She'd been a blind fool to think herself in love with Carl Jamieson. When their relationship had involved easily arranged fun times, he'd been an absolute charmer, but he'd had neither any empathy nor patience with her decision to help her parents keep their home. All he'd cared about had been the inconvenience to him and the restrictions it would place on their sex life. He'd only *loved* her because she'd fitted in with *his* needs, and when that wasn't going to happen all the time, it was 'Goodbye, Daisy'.

She could see their relationship more clearly now. At the beginning she'd been enormously flattered by Carl's interest in her—a handsome, *with-it* guy, forging a successful career in computer technology. What did he want with an ordinary girl like her? She was reasonably attractive, reasonably intelligent, a capable kind of person, but nothing special. But that, of course, had made her the perfect choice for Carl—someone eager to fall in with whatever he wanted, someone who didn't outshine or compete with him, who thought he was wonderful…until he showed that he wasn't.

He'd wanted an easy, uncomplicated partner who would always put him first, and she had, oh, so willingly done that until her parents' problems had rearranged her priorities and proved to her beyond any doubt that Carl was not the kind of man to be counted on in a crisis and definitely not someone she would want to marry. Even so, the hurt and disillusionment of the break-up had lingered on, making her disinterested in men in general.

Especially handsome men who always put what they wanted above every other consideration.

It certainly wouldn't be good for her to get interested in Ethan Cartwright, she fiercely told herself. Nevertheless, he had shown enough concern for her crisis to give her this job, which gave some credit to his character. On the other hand, he could well afford it, so maybe not too much credit. Paying her salary was probably only a drop in the bucket to him, totally negligible. However, her own pride insisted she earn it as best she could and it was about time she set about doing something active instead of churning over feelings that had nothing to do with work.

Anxious to be in hearing distance when the chandelier people and the architect called at the house, she remained inside, taking up Ethan Cartwright's invitation to check out the rest of the rooms. He'd set up a computer work station in his office. The utility room was already furnished with a washing machine and clothes dryer, ready for his use. She noticed there was a handy chute in one corner for dirty clothes to be dropped down from upstairs. Very convenient. The powder room under the staircase was positively luxurious—mostly gleaming white with artistic touches of black and silver.

The bedrooms upstairs were huge compared to most modern standards, all of them with built-in cupboards and en suite bathrooms. The master suite, which was the only one furnished and obviously being used, was enormous. Not only did it have its own private bathroom with a jacuzzi and a shower big enough for two, but a large dressing room, as well.

Daisy could hardly believe there was nothing out of place in any of these rooms. No towels left on the floor, no toiletries sprawled over the vanity bench in the bathroom where she could still smell the lingering scent of his aftershave cologne, which undoubtedly occupied a shelf in the mirrored cupboard above the vanity bench. She didn't look for it, uneasy enough about this much intrusion of privacy.

It felt weirdly intimate just staring at the colour co-ordinated rows of clothes in his dressing room, with the matching shoes precisely lined up in specially made racks below them. It had surprised her that his bed had been made, not left in disarray, but all this…was Ethan Cartwright obsessively neat or did he simply like everything in order?

Daisy shook her head in sheer bemusement. She'd never known a man who wasn't messy—her brothers, her father, past boyfriends, Carl in particular, stepping out of their clothes, leaving them on the floor, piling dirty dishes in the sink, shoes being dropped wherever they took them off. They didn't actually expect a woman to clean up after them. Mess didn't seem to bother them. She wondered why Ethan Cartwright was different.

Even the kitchen had been absolutely pristine, though he must have made himself some breakfast since he was living here. All the stainless-steel appliances had been gleaming and there hadn't been so much as a wipe smear on the black granite bench tops. Curiosity drove her downstairs to check his pantry. Sure enough the shelves were packed in precise order, sauces and spices lined up for easy access, other staples grouped together. It was certainly the most efficient way to organise a kitchen. Maybe he was a genius at time and motion.

Daisy couldn't help being impressed by this aspect of his character. She was a bit of a neat freak herself, liking to know where everything was so she didn't get frustrated hunting for mislaid items, wasting time that wouldn't need to be wasted if a bit more care was taken in the first place. But maybe he was a control freak, which wouldn't be easy to live with. She had to stop thinking things that added to an attraction that was already too disturbingly strong.

The doorbell was a welcome distraction.

It was the architect.

'Hi! I'm Charlie Hollier and I presume you're Daisy Donahue,' he rattled out with a broad smile. 'Ethan called me and said you'd be here.'

'Right!' She smiled back. He was short and stocky, not much taller than her, with a rather homely face and friendly blue eyes twinkling at her as though he was happy to make her acquaintance. The fact that he was wearing blue jeans and a blue-and-white checked sports shirt also made Daisy feel immediately relaxed with him.

'He mentioned you suggested a bar in the games room. Good idea! Should have thought of it myself. We won't have to wait until the end of a game to go and get a drink from the kitchen.'

'You're one of his Tuesday group?'

He nodded. 'Always a great night. Let's go and have a look where best to put it.'

They walked inside to survey the situation. Daisy could not contain her curiosity. 'How many of you come to play?'

'Well, there's the old solid core from Riverview. Ethan and Mickey started it amongst the boarders in our class when we were at school together. A bit of competitive fun when we weren't at sport or study. That's three regulars plus Mickey when he's in town, and other friends we've made since then. Usually we have eight people turn up, sometimes more.'

Riverview…it was one of the big private schools at Hunters Hill, sited just across the Lane Cove River from this house. Being a boarder probably meant each student had allotted spaces for his possessions and he would certainly be disciplined into making his bed. If Ethan Cartwright had spent the six years of secondary school there, that could have become habitual, and it would be fairly natural for him to have a place for everything and everything kept in its place—nothing too odd about it.

Daisy was bursting to ask more questions about Ethan Cartwright's personal life, but reined in what could be seen as too much interest from a mere employee.

The architect decided on a corner bar next to the wall that backed onto the utility room—easy to run plumbing for a sink through from there. He would amend the plans and give a new set to Daisy so she could keep an eye on everything and stop mistakes from being made. 'I'm delighted Ethan has found someone to be on the spot all the time,' he added enthusiastically. 'You'd be surprised how often things have to be fixed because they weren't done right in the first place.'

Daisy was relieved to hear this. It made her feel she could be of real value here, earning her salary.

'In fact, I'd appreciate it—Ethan would, too—if you'd ensure that the men laying the slate around the pool today get the mix right,' Charlie ran on as they strolled out to the back of the house where the work was going on. 'Quite a lot of the slate will be charcoal-grey without the blue-green streaks in it. Sometimes they just reach for the next piece of slate in the pile and you end up with a square metre of all grey instead of splashes of colour here and there.'

'Okay. I'll keep an eye on that,' Daisy promised, feeling better and better about the job.

They toured the whole site together with Charlie checking on progress, Daisy listening to how he wanted everything to be. 'It seems a bit weird to me that all this is just for one person,' she couldn't help commenting as they returned to the house.

'Actually Ethan was planning to get married when he bought the place,' Charlie tossed off casually. 'Changed his mind, thank God!'

She shot him a quizzical look. 'You didn't like the woman?'

He grimaced. 'A bit too much into being the lady of the manor for my liking. But I'm glad Ethan decided to keep the manor anyway. It's going to be fantastic when it's all finished.'

'It certainly is,' she agreed, terribly tempted to pump more out of Charlie about *the woman*, but that was none of her business and it should remain none of her business.

Nevertheless, the phrase—lady of the manor— conjured up someone stunningly beautiful with all the airs and graces learnt from an exclusive finishing school where manners were polished and deportment and elocution were perfected. No doubt she had been trained to be the wife of a billionaire, knowing how to hostess every social event and look the part with elegant ease. Ethan Cartwright would naturally choose to marry a woman like that. She wondered what had happened to change his mind about the one he had chosen.

The lighting people arrived soon after the architect had left. As she watched the chandelier being carefully lowered onto the canvas laid out on the floor, it was impossible not to feel a pang of regret at its removal even though it wouldn't suit the lifestyle Ethan planned for himself. Perhaps the lady of the manor had wanted to keep the grandeur of the old house and they'd clashed on that point, realising they'd envisaged different futures together.

Whatever…it was none of her business.

She had a job to do and she would do it to the best of her ability.

Ethan was frustrated. Almost three weeks had passed and he was getting nowhere with Daisy Donahue. What he needed was a good block of time with her—enough time to get past the business of the day and onto more promising ground.

She was gone when he arrived home after work, always leaving him a note on what had been accomplished during the day, informing him of any snags to the flow of progress and how and when they would be corrected. Each morning she arrived all fresh and perky at eight o'clock, provoking an instant rush of sexual excitement, but no matter how long he delayed his departure, she would not be diverted from talk about the job. It was as though she was obsessed with it, not the least bit interested in him as a man, quickly brushing past every attempt he made at a more personal connection.

Nevertheless, the interest was there. He felt it in the tense way she deliberately kept a physical distance between them. He saw it in an occasional flash of her eyes before her gaze quickly slid away from his. He actually sensed her inward battle to suppress it whenever she was in his company.

It was obvious that she needed to feel secure in the position of his on-site project manager, continually affirming that her salary was being earned. Having a regular income was a big issue with her and she was probably determined not to risk losing it by indulging an attraction that could rock her boat.

I don't gamble.

Somehow that steely will had to be broken.

Or at least bent.

His way.

Daisy always rang the doorbell when she arrived at the Hunters Hill mansion each morning. Although she had a set of house keys and could have let herself in, the solid common sense of keeping everything formal between her and Ethan Cartwright stopped her from taking any kind of familiar freedom on his territory when he was at home.

He'd greeted her at the door one morning wearing only a short black silk wrap-around robe. Even though he had been decently covered, the deep V of bared chest with the sprinkle of black, curly hair and the powerful muscularity of his long legs had messed with her head for the rest of the day. No way did she want to catch him by surprise in any state of undress. The man oozed masculine sexuality. The more she saw of him, the more he rattled all her female hormones.

Even when she'd believed herself in love with Carl, he hadn't affected her like this—such a strong physical tug that inspired lustful thoughts. Sex with Carl had been more a natural progression of romance, not some primitive form of sheer wantonness that kept pleading for connection, eroding the common sense she had to hang onto.

She *knew* Ethan Cartwright was too much of a high flyer to ever consider her as a possible wife. She wasn't beautiful. She had no outstanding talent to lift her above her very ordinary background. Her circumstances were such that she was no match for him on any level, and no match meant no serious relationship.

Playing with her…that was something altogether different. She strongly suspected he enjoyed doing that already and wanted to push it further, but since Daisy couldn't see herself becoming *the main event* in his life, pride wouldn't allow her to fall into the role of a bit on the side, not even for the satisfaction of knowing what it would be like to have an intimate connection with him.

Most likely this was a case of her being on the spot and him not having chosen another sexual partner since breaking up with his fiancée. He probably viewed her as a nice little tonic for his hurt pride—a good dose and he'd feel on top of his world again. Which would make Daisy just another feather stuffed in his winner's cap. Her self-esteem insisted she was worth more than that. She'd been used once. She wasn't going to be used again. Despite the fact that Ethan Cartwright left Carl for dead in the attraction stakes.

As she rang the doorbell on Thursday morning of the third week of working for him, Daisy was thinking she had to find a new job. Fast. With a boss who didn't agitate her so *physically* and make her dream impossible dreams.

The door opened and she was confronted by another strong blast of sex appeal, though at least it was encased—enhanced?—by a superbly tailored business suit. 'Ah, Daisy!' Ethan Cartwright rolled out in his rich voice. 'I have a special task for you today.'

The twinkling anticipation in his gorgeous green eyes made her heart flutter. She had difficulty catching enough breath to produce a querying 'Oh?'

He flashed a teasing grin. 'You're so good at leaving me lists of things to note, I thought you'd appreciate getting a list from me. It's in the kitchen. Come on in.'

He set off down the hallway and she followed him at a safe distance, fiercely telling herself not to get besotted by a silly grin. Despite this stern resolve, her stomach was mush and her pulse was pounding at her temples so distractingly her mind barely registered the words he tossed back at her.

'You know the tennis court people and the guys who've done such a great job with the swimming pool…' he cast a sparkling glance back at her '…with your eagle eye upon them will all be finishing up tomorrow.'

She nodded.

'Well, I thought I'd give them a barbecue lunch in appreciation of the fine work they've done,' he continued cheerfully. 'Send them off with good feelings so they'll be happy to return if any problem arises.'

'You want me to do it?' Daisy asked, not expecting him to be on hand during the day.

'No. I want you to shop for it today and help me with the preparation tomorrow morning. I'll do the cooking.'

Surprise tripped her into saying, 'You're going to feed a group of tradesmen yourself?'

He paused at the kitchen doorway, shooting her a quizzical look. 'Why not?'

She almost bumped into him. Heat flooded into her cheeks as she reared back a step, wishing she could evade the riveting intensity of his eyes, but determined not to appear even more disturbed by him than she had already revealed. Since it was impossible to voice her assumption that *he* wouldn't mix socially with ordinary people when he obviously planned to, she had to come up with something else.

'I thought you'd be occupied with your important clients.'

He lifted a hand, featherlight fingertips grazing her hot skin. 'Everyone is important, Daisy,' he said softly, his eyes smiling at her confusion. 'And I believe in rewarding good work.'

Her heart was thundering. She couldn't tear her gaze away from the caring in his, or her face away from his mesmerising touch. She liked him. She really, really liked him. And she wanted...but she couldn't let herself want that.

'Right!' she managed to mutter.

For a long, long, moment he said nothing. Her toes curled with tension. Her mind whirled with dangerous possibilities. What if he stepped forward and kissed her? What would she feel? The terrible part was she didn't want to resist if he did make the move and that could land her in all sorts of trouble.

'Right!' he finally repeated, and with a quickly sucked-in breath added, 'Let's get to the list.'

Daisy sucked in quite a few quick breaths herself as she followed him into the kitchen, sensibly walking around to the other side of the island bench to put it between them. She was still shaking inside from that moment of aching vulnerability and was intensely grateful to have the list to look at as Ethan went through it with her, explaining what he intended to do with everything. The wives of three of the men would also be coming, he informed her, so there would be twelve people to feed, including herself and Ethan.

'Just add anything you think would be good,' he said,

pulling a wad of notes from his wallet. 'This should cover everything.'

She frowned at the amount of money he was trusting her with. 'I'll bring home the dockets and give you the change tomorrow.'

His mouth quirked in amusement. 'I'm sure you'll account for every cent.'

'It's what I'm used to doing,' she shot at him with a touch of belligerence, needing to emphasise the difference between them for her own sake. He could afford to splash money around as much as he liked whereas she…she started to wonder if he would use leftovers or let her take them home at the end of the day.

He immediately changed the subject. 'Do you play tennis, Daisy?'

'Yes,' popped out of her mouth before she thought where that question might be leading.

'Good!' His smile smacked of wicked satisfaction. 'Bring your tennis gear with you. And your swimming costume. I've already spoken to the men about trying out the pool and having a game of tennis. Should be a fun afternoon.'

Fun?

It might be for him, but it wouldn't be for her.

Her mind boggled at the thought of seeing Ethan Cartwright in nothing but a swimming costume. It was bad enough being trapped into spending a whole day in proximity with this treacherously attractive man. She could only hope he wore surfboard shorts.

'Have to leave now,' he ran on, tapping the list. 'Are you okay with this?'

'Yes. Have a good day!' she rattled out, relieved that she was not going to be mentally and physically buffeted by his presence any longer. At least, not today. Tomorrow was looming as an exercise of intense discipline over her mind and body with him around all the time.

Tomorrow…it was like a song of glorious promise in Ethan's mind as he drove towards the city centre. There'd been a moment this morning when he'd almost given in to the temptation to kiss her until she melted against him, the heat in her cheeks coursing through both of them in a firestorm of desire. He'd imagined sweeping her up in his arms, carrying her up the staircase to his bed, ravishing her until she gave up everything she was to him.

Only the constraints of time had stopped him. He had an important business meeting this morning. But tomorrow he'd manipulate a situation where she couldn't deny the strong connection that had unmistakably pulsed between them in the hallway. One way or another he was going to persuade Daisy Donahue to surrender to it with all the intensity of passion he'd felt vibrating from her since the moment they'd met.

CHAPTER SIX

WHEN Ethan opened the door to Daisy on Friday morning, he was wearing black shorts, a black sports shirt with white trim around the collar, black-and-white tennis shoes with black socks. The athletic style of the man in these clothes instantly raised his sex appeal which was already far too high for Daisy's peace of mind.

He gave her appearance a quick cursory glance—a loose blue-and-white striped T-shirt over knee-length white shorts—a sensible, sexless outfit—and his mouth quirked with ironic amusement as though he knew she had deliberately dressed down. For one stomach-churning moment challenge simmered in his green eyes, but he simply greeted her normally, then stood back and waved her inside.

'The men are rigging up the sails which will shade the barbecue dining area,' he informed her as they headed down the hallway. 'The tennis court is getting a last vacuum before the net goes up. Everything should be ready by the time the wives arrive after dropping their children at school. We have about an hour and a half to prepare all the food before taking on the host and hostess roles. Are you okay with that?'

'Yes,' she answered, only too grateful that she could soon busy herself with other people.

It was good to be busy in the kitchen, as well, helping Ethan prepare the salads, cutting up onions to accompany the steak and sausages, spreading garlic butter on the loaves of French bread.

'I see you're used to doing this kind of catering,' he remarked after they'd been working together for a while.

'Family parties. We all get together at Easter and Christmas,' she explained with a shrug.

'You have a big family?'

'Three older brothers and one older sister. All married with children. I was the accident. Mum was forty when she had me.'

'And how old are you?'

'Twenty-seven.'

'No marriage in view as yet?'

'No.'

'Boyfriend?'

She frowned at him. 'That's a very personal question.'

He shrugged. 'You've been working for me for three weeks and I realise I hardly know anything about you, Daisy. Not even where you live.'

'I live at Ryde with my parents.'

'To save money, no doubt.'

She flashed him a grim look at his quick understanding. 'Yes, a fact that my last boyfriend didn't appreciate.'

'Ah!' His mouth twitched into a satisfied little smile.

Daisy was vexed with herself for letting that slip. If Ethan Cartwright was thinking she was free for fun and games, he could think again. She was not about to waste her time and emotion on a man who would dump her when he found another lady for the manor. She chopped up a cucumber with extra vigour.

'How did your parents get into debt?'

The question surprised her, stirring a hope that he might toss out some free financial advice. She arranged her mouth into a rueful smile and looked directly at him as she answered. 'Their superannuation manager directed them into investments which had gone bad. They borrowed money from the bank to renovate their home, believing they would have enough income to service the loan…'

'And then the bottom fell out of the market,' he finished for her. 'Unfortunately a fairly common problem these days.'

It was an offhand dismissal of the subject. Daisy gritted her teeth over the stupid hope, then with a touch of resentment asked, 'How is it that you knew better?'

'My father is an economist,' he answered matter-of-factly. 'He was forecasting this financial blow-up for years. For the most part it didn't suit people to listen to him. Many wrote him off as a crackpot academic.'

'But you didn't.'

He shook his head. 'Numbers don't lie. Numbers made the crash inevitable.'

She wished she could ask him to look at her parents' investment portfolio, tell them where best to put what was left of their money, but such expert advice was his business. It wouldn't come free and even if she could afford his fees, it would still smack of asking him for a favour, taking on an extra client whose nest-egg wouldn't be big enough to earn him much of a commission. Favours put people under obligation to return them and she had nothing to offer Ethan Cartwright.

Except…

No, don't go there, she sternly told herself.

Giving in to sexual chemistry was one thing.

Wanting financial pillow-talk out of it was something else.

But he'd be using her so why shouldn't she use him?

The idea of having sex with him had been squirrelling around in her mind for weeks. She *wanted* to know how it would feel. He was, without a doubt, the most attractive man she'd ever met. It was only natural to be tempted to have the experience even though it wouldn't lead to a serious relationship, and if there were side benefits…at least that would make up for being dumped afterwards. She could come out winning.

On the other hand, that was a gamble and she didn't gamble.

The higher probability was she would come out losing…losing this job before she could find another, losing her self-esteem, losing her sense of right and wrong, and it was certainly wrong to barter sex for help. This wasn't exactly a survival situation. She could manage it by herself. But for how long? And at what cost to her own life?

Heaving a despondent sigh, she picked up the punnet of cherry tomatoes and started cutting them in half to add to the green salad. *He* was whipping up a home-made dressing, blending Spanish onion with vinegar, sugar, vegetable oil, water, salt and mustard. The blender was switched off long enough for him to dip a finger into the mixture and lift that finger to his mouth for tasting.

Her heart did a ridiculous flip. It wasn't a deliber-ately erotic action. Although when he saw her looking at him, those devilish green eyes sparkled wickedly. The urgent need for some down-to-earth distraction made her grab at the first non-sexual thought that ran through her mind.

'How come you're so into cooking?' she blurted out.

'I enjoy eating well. Don't you?'

'Yes. But you could afford to frequent the best restaurants. You don't have to do it yourself.'

'There's more satisfaction in doing it precisely to one's own taste. My grandmother taught me that.'

'Your grandmother?'

He grinned, delighted to have teased her interest. 'From the time I was a boy hanging out in her kitchen. I used to go there after school. She loved cooking and everything I ate with her tasted so much better than the stuff my parents bought. Neither of them ever cooked. It was always frozen meals or takeaways, eaten in an absent-minded fashion whenever they felt the need for fuel. They're both so wrapped up in their mental world, the physical world barely impinges on it.'

He must have had a strange upbringing, Daisy thought, very different from her family life. 'Does that mean your mother is an academic, too?' she asked, unable to squash her curiosity about him.

He nodded. 'The law is her life. She lectures on it at university. Writes books on it.'

'Were you an only child?' He hadn't indicated the presence of any siblings.

'One was enough for my parents,' he said dryly. 'Not that they didn't care for me. They did in their own way. Though I'd have to say the best thing they did for me was send me to boarding school. I had a great time at Riverview with Mickey and Charlie and the other guys.'

He poured the dressing into a sauce-boat ready to use later. 'Though the food wasn't up to my grandmother's standard,' he added ruefully. 'When I finally struck out on my own, I wanted to cook for myself.'

Daisy had to agree it was hard to beat a really good home-cooked meal.

'This dressing is one of my grandmother's recipes,' he ran on. 'Have a taste.'

It was impossible to resist dipping a finger in and carrying it to her mouth, though she was conscious of him watching the action, waiting for her response. 'Mmm…yummy.'

He laughed. 'It's always a pleasure to share pleasures.'

His eyes twinkled with a seductive invitation to share many more with him.

Daisy instantly pulled herself back into a defensive shell. Everything about Ethan Cartwright made him too temptingly attractive. It was becoming more and more difficult to hang onto common sense. She couldn't even write him off as a selfish, arrogant pig any more. He didn't act like one.

But there was still the huge barrier of his billionaire status, and she couldn't help resenting how easily he could throw money around, getting absolutely everything he wanted. Somehow that made it all the more imperative that he shouldn't get her, not as anything but an employee who fairly earned her wage.

Ethan observed the shut-down on her face and the belligerent set of her chin as she finished with the tomatoes and moved to the tray where she'd placed the cutlery wrapped in paper serviettes.

'I'll take this down to the barbecue area, save having to bring it later,' she slung at him, avoiding eye contact, and was off, not waiting for him to agree or disagree.

She moved so fast, her pony-tail and her perky bottom twitched from side to side. Ethan grinned to himself, sure that it had become too hot in the kitchen for her and she was taking evasive action. She was so marvellously different from the women who virtually threw themselves at him. With Daisy there was no flirting to encourage his interest, and a swift back-pedalling whenever she felt herself teetering on the brink of responding to him beyond her set limits.

All the no-go signs from her only served to make the challenge of breaking through her barriers more compelling. He had made some headway this morning, moving onto personal ground, drawing out a curiosity about his life which revealed the interest she'd been deliberately repressing.

Maybe her ex-boyfriend had soured her view of men generally and she was wary of letting herself be vulnerable again. Certainly his experience with Serena had reinforced his cynical view of women. But he felt the potential for something very different with Daisy Donahue and nothing was going to stop him from clinching a connection with her. He had the rest of the day to work on cracking her resistance to being with him.

Daisy threw herself into the role of party hostess, determined to avoid being with Ethan Cartwright as much as possible. Luckily, none of the wives played tennis, so she couldn't be drawn into playing a set of mixed doubles. The morning passed agreeably enough. The women expressed interest in a tour of the mansion and with Ethan's permission, she showed them all they wanted to see, then stayed chatting with them at poolside, only moving away to refill drinks and ensure everyone was enjoying themselves.

All the men either played tennis or watched the game, amusing themselves with a lively commentary on the play, then cooling off in the pool before lunch. Daisy was the only one who didn't go into the water, escaping to the kitchen on the pretext of last-minute preparations for the barbecue.

The vision of Ethan Cartwright in a brief black swimming costume had made her so hotly conscious of her own body, no way was she about to don the bikini she had brought with her. It was far more comfortable sticking her head into the refrigerator, staring at the contents which were largely dead meat with no sex appeal whatsoever. She was still blankly looking at the tray loaded with steak and sausages when *his* voice assaulted her ears with a tone of extreme annoyance.

'This is totally absurd! You have no reason whatsoever to act as though I'm Lynda Twiggley, demanding that you toe some tyrannical line of duty every second of the day. I will not have it!'

It jerked her around to face a dripping-wet splendid male physique emanating a savage energy that sent wild quivers through her entire system. He'd slid open one of the glass doors that led onto the back verandah and stood just outside the dining area, glowering at her with fierce green eyes.

'I told you to bring a swimming costume,' he ranted on. 'You know I wanted you to join in the fun. There is no need for you to be up here fussing over food. Since you must be perfectly aware of that I find it distinctly of-fensive that you choose to turn your back on the rest of us…'

The accusation flustered Daisy into rushing out an apology. 'I'm sorry. I didn't mean to give offence. I was just…'

'Just nothing!' He pointed to her beach bag which she'd dropped at the end of the island bench. 'If that contains what it should contain, get changed and be down at the pool within five minutes. This is play time, Daisy. I expect my staff to follow the agenda I set.'

Having delivered this blistering ultimatum, Ethan strode off to return to his guests. The shock of his anger and the implied threat to her job had Daisy scuttling for her beach bag the moment his back was turned. She raced into the powder room under the staircase, threw off her clothes, dragged on her bikini bottom and fastened the bra top as fast as her fingers could work.

A glimpse in the mirror made her feel dreadfully naked and hopelessly vulnerable. She was too ac-cessible to Ethan's touch and if he did touch her, she was frightened of showing him some uncontrollable response, and he'd know he could get to her physically, know and probably take advantage of it.

Any confidence in maintaining a proper distance between them was shot to pieces. Never had she felt so gut-wrenchingly nervous about wearing a bikini. Never. Ever. She wasn't ashamed of her body. It was slim enough and curvy enough to wear a bikini reasonably well, but how could she hide the effect Ethan had on her with only a few scraps of material for cover? It was no shield at all. It left her terribly, terribly defenceless.

Her frantic mind screamed there was no time to

worry about this. About three minutes had already gone and her job was at stake. Snatching up the towel from her bag, she ran to the door Ethan had left open and kept running, heading straight for the pool, not looking at anything but the water ahead of her, desperately blanking her mind to the fear of revealing far more than her almost-naked body.

A cheer went up from some of the men at the sight of her flying figure stripped of its usual cover-up clothes. Daisy didn't let herself think or care what they thought. She dropped her towel on the slate patio and dived in, staying under the surface of the water until she reached the other side of the pool and had to come up for air. Having taken a few deep breaths to calm her pounding heart, she swam slowly to the steps at the shallow end where the other women were sitting, paddling their feet.

'Love your red bikini,' one of them said, smiling at her.

'Can't wear one any more,' another remarked ruefully. 'Having babies gave me an awful jelly belly.'

'Why not consider cosmetic surgery if you feel bad about it?' the third woman suggested.

This topic was instantly bandied around. Daisy sat on the middle step in waist-deep water, letting the conversation float around her, trying very hard to appear calm and at home with the party scene. It gradually dawned on her that it hadn't worried the women that she'd gone missing. They were older than she was, comfortable in each other's company with the many experiences of motherhood to share. They seemed to view their men as children, too, happy to sit apart and relax on the sidelines while indulgently watching their husbands at play.

Maybe the tradesmen had made some joking remarks to Ethan about her conscientious devotion to duty, suggesting he loosen the work-rein on her today, possibly implying she deserved some time off. The niggling criticism would have irked him, given that she was supposed to be enjoying the party with them. Whatever…she had to be careful not to arouse his displeasure again.

The problem was in not being able to act normally around him. He made her so tense all the time, having to fight the attraction he exerted on her. She should probably check where he was, try to judge from his expression if her swift response to his angry command had mollified the offence she had given. On the other hand, if she just sat here quietly, keeping her attention on the women, she shouldn't get into any more trouble.

'Daisy…'

Her nerves instantly twitched at the sound of Ethan's voice, but at least there was no sharp edge to it this time. The tone held quite a pleasant lilt and she quickly constructed an inquiring smile as she turned in response to the call.

He stood halfway along the side of the pool, beckoning to her, obviously intent on a private tête-à-tête. It meant she had to get out of the water and go to meet him, wearing nothing but a dripping-wet bikini since she'd left her towel on the other side of the pool and she didn't dare keep him waiting while she went and picked it up.

'What's it like working for such a gorgeous hunk?' one of the women slung at her curiously as Daisy rose to her feet and started up the steps.

Difficult almost slipped off her tongue. The spectre

of Lynda Twiggley blasting her for indiscretion rattled her just in time. She flashed a smile at the woman, quickly answering, 'He's actually very kind, very generous.'

'Then you've got a brilliant package there.' An encouraging grin was thrown back at her. 'You should go for him, Daisy.'

She shook her head. 'Not a good idea. But right now I have to go *to* him, so please excuse me.'

The women laughed at her quip and she left them to their own amusement, forcing her legs to walk around the pool to the man who was, indeed, brilliantly packaged, and the *gorgeous hunk* part of the package was very much on display. It didn't matter how sternly she told herself not to find him desirable. She did. Any woman would.

He had the physical perfection of Michelangelo's *David*, every masculine muscle shining under taut, tanned skin, vibrantly alive, not carved in cold white marble. Ethan Cartwright, wearing only a brief scrap of black fabric that seemed like a brazen pouch exhibiting even more sexual power, was hot, hot, hot, and just the sight of him made her own blood race with heat. It was impossible to control the response he drew from her.

Her heart thumped. Her stomach fluttered. She was acutely conscious of her bare thighs rubbing together as she walked towards him. And worst of all, with his gaze directly on her approach, taking in the full vision of *her* body in the red bikini, she felt her nipples tightening into hard bullets with no way of hiding that fact under a wet bra. It was difficult to resist the urge to fold her arms against her chest. Reason insisted that action would only emphasise her self-consciousness and a stiff bolt of pride refused to give into such obvious weakness.

Nevertheless, anxiety rushed her into speech the moment she was close enough to him not to be over-heard. 'Have I done something else wrong?'

His far too sensual mouth moved into an ironic grimace. 'No. I want to apologise for being so curt with you. I didn't mean to frighten you into acting like a scalded cat. Your job here is not at risk, Daisy. I just don't want you to be scarred by your experience with Lynda Twiggley. It won't hurt you to be more relaxed with me.'

'No. Okay,' she agreed, relieved that he was no longer annoyed with her. To be absolutely sure of not making another mistake, she asked, 'What is the agenda now?'

He waved towards the group of men at the other end of the pool. 'The guys and I are about to start the bar-becue and put the meat on. Why not rustle up the ladies to help bring down the salads and generally get ready for lunch? No hurry. Keep it casual and friendly.'

'Will do,' she promised.

'They'll all be gone by three o'clock. Children to be picked up from school and an early start to the weekend for the men. Since you missed out on a game of tennis this morning, I'll play a set with you then.' He gave her a cheerful grin. 'Can't have you bringing a tennis racquet for nothing.'

He tossed these last words at her as he started strol-ling back to the barbecue area, leaving Daisy open-mouthed, struggling for a protest or an excuse to escape playing with him—being alone with him. She had the sinking feeling he would accept neither, anyway.

He wasn't going to let her off.

She would have to play the set of tennis.

Maybe she could surprise him by beating him. He didn't know she was an A-grade player. If his male ego got hurt, that might make him a lot less attractive. And he might not want to play with her any more. In any sense.

It was the only hope she could hold onto for staying on here without this constant feeling of vulnerability where he was concerned. She had to beat him this afternoon. Had to.

CHAPTER SEVEN

EVERYONE had helped clean up after the party before leaving. There was nothing for Daisy to do except play tennis with Ethan. At least both of them had changed back into their morning clothes so she didn't have such an acute physical awareness to distract her. As they strolled down to the court, she tried to keep the conversation between them light and natural, commenting on the guests' enjoyment of the day, pretending to be completely relaxed.

The tennis court was blue with a green surround and a high green wire fence to keep in wayward balls. 'Were you pleased with the surface when you played this morning?' she asked on their way down the flight of steps to it.

'Yes. No bumps anywhere. No odd bounces. They've done a great job with it.'

'I didn't watch the game.' She shot him an arch look. 'Are you terribly good? Will you wipe me off the court?'

He laughed, shaking his head. 'You're quite safe. I'll play to whatever your standard is, Daisy.'

She didn't *feel* safe, not from the attraction that was

so difficult to squash. However, his promise to accommodate her tennis standard did give her the chance to beat him. Hopefully that would be a hit to the ego that had just assumed he was the better player and he'd be so put out he wouldn't want to play other games with her.

'I think you should serve first so I can judge for myself,' she said, anticipating that he would go easy on her to begin with.

'As you like.'

He put down a medium-paced serve which any reasonable player could return and Daisy suspected he deliberately over-hit the ball to let her win the first rally. On the second point she cunningly sidelined him, laughingly declaring it was a lucky shot. The third point was more seriously contested and she was relieved when he netted the ball, giving her three game points. She managed to win one of them with a drop shot he wasn't expecting, which gave her the first game.

'Hmmm...' His green eyes were twinkling suspiciously as they crossed at the net. 'Am I playing with a closet professional?'

'How can you even imagine that?' She grinned at him. 'I never shriek or grunt when I hit the ball.'

She sliced her first serve so wide it was ungettable. She put her second serve down the T, leaving him standing again. He netted her third serve. The fourth he managed to return in court, but his shot was high enough for her to smash a winner from it. Two games to love. It was a great start.

He walked up to the net, no longer under any delusion that she was an easy beat. 'Where do you usually play?'

'At the Chatswood Tennis Club.'

'How often?'

'Most Saturday afternoons.'

Until the annual membership fee became due again. She couldn't risk paying it, not when her job future was still so uncertain and every dollar earned might be important. Her tennis-playing days could soon be over for a long while, but today she was still in good form and very grateful for it.

'A-grade?' Ethan asked.

'Yes.'

He suddenly grinned, which wasn't the reaction Daisy needed to get from him. 'What do they call you? The pocket rocket?'

'No. Just Daisy.'

He shook his head in bemusement. 'I wouldn't call you *just* anything, Daisy Donahue. Compared to all the other women of my acquaintance, you are, without a doubt, the most remarkable.'

The compliment went straight to her head like champagne. The fizz of pleasure completely undermined the wish to bruise his ego. Besides, it didn't seem possible in the light of his amazing admiration. He should be in a snit over being made to look inadequate against her, but he wasn't. His voice held a relish for the competition as he tossed 'Game on!' at her.

She watched him stroll back to the service line, no lack of confidence in his bearing. She couldn't help thinking he was the most remarkable man of her acquaintance and she was riven with the temptation to simply go with the flow of attraction wherever it took her. Which would probably be terribly foolish, given her job situation, not to mention the huge difference in their stations in life.

However, both these factors lost all significance in the intensely fought contest that followed the revelation of her ability to play at a highly challenging standard. Ethan stormed through his next service game. She had to fight hard to keep hers. It felt as though every point was an exhilarating win or an anguished loss. He had the greater strength but Daisy was a well-practised tactician and she refused to let his power dominate.

Ethan applauded every particularly skilful shot she made. There was no acrimony at all coming from him, more a bubbling delight running through the banter he carried on at the change of ends, making the game even more stimulating, mentally and physically. Daisy loved every minute of it, loved playing with him, loved the contest of wits and skill and the sweet thrill of his admiring comments. He was gorgeous, marvellous, and it was like a cocktail of sheer joy to be his match on the tennis court.

He gradually won his way back to six games all, then insisted they play a tie-breaker to decide the victor. Somehow beating him didn't seem important any more, although Daisy still fought hard to take the set. He delivered a fantastic backhand to triumph in the end, and she dropped her racquet to applaud it, wanting to fairly acknowledge the great shot.

In uninhibited joy he leapt over the net, tossed his racquet on top of hers, and before she could even imagine what he intended, he swept her into his embrace, grinning wickedly as he declared, 'Winner takes the prize.'

He kissed her.

Her heart was still banging away from the exertion of their last rally. Her body was hot. So was his. Whether it was the energy drain of the game, being taken by surprise or the sudden wild surge of need to know him like this, resistance was simply beyond Daisy at that moment. Her arms automatically lifted and wound themselves around his neck, and she kissed him back.

Ethan swiftly took advantage of her surrender to his seductive sensuality, changing his kiss to one of driving passion, tightening his embrace, clamping her lower body to his, and Daisy was bombarded by so many exciting sensations, it was totally impossible to extract herself from them. The desire she'd tried so hard to hold in check burst through her in a raging compulsion to experience all of him.

Her fingers spread into his hair, clasping his head as her mouth ravaged his as intensely as his ravaged hers. Her breasts, pressed so hard against the hot heaving wall of his chest, tingled with wild sensitivity. His hands curled around her bottom, lifting her into a more intimate physical connection. She was acutely aware of his erection furrowing her stomach. It didn't set off warning signals in her mind. She revelled in his desire for her, the excitement of it consuming all common sense.

With dizzying speed, he broke off their kiss, scooped her up in his arms and was carrying her, striding off the tennis court, mounting the steps to the pool terrace. Her arms were locked around his neck. She didn't think of questioning his action. She was madly exulting in his strength. Never had a man made her feel so marvellously *taken*, as though she really was a prize. It was incredibly heady stuff and she nestled her face against his throat, breathing in the intoxicating male scent of him.

He charged into the pool cabana. There was a bed in the back room. A last thread of sanity screamed that she should stop him now, but she didn't want to. Her whole being yearned to let this happen, to indulge the desire to have Ethan Cartwright, to feel everything he could make her feel. She was twenty-seven years old and no other man had ever affected her so intensely. Her swirling mind rebelled against sanity, against pride, against everything that should stand in the way of letting herself be swept into bed with him.

He stood her on her feet, whipped off her T-shirt and removed her bra in a few breathless seconds. His shirt was discarded just as fast and she was barely conscious of her own semi-nakedness, being so entranced with his. He was beautiful, magnificent, and what she had thought of as untouchable was suddenly there to be touched and she didn't even have to reach out because Ethan hauled her back into his embrace and was kissing her again, making the excitement of her bared soft flesh pressed against the muscle-toned heat of his even more lusty.

Her hands slid greedily over his powerful shoulders, loving the taut smooth skin, the sense of great strength, of an energy force that was pouring into passion for her. The sheer animal pleasure of feeling him like this completely banished any restraint. She touched everything she could reach—his back, his ears, his thick, silky hair, wildly revelling in the freedom from every inhibition.

He moved her with him to the bed. They tumbled onto it, still kissing each other with a fierce hunger for all they could take from this coming together. He tore his mouth from hers, heaved himself down to kiss her breasts with a hot urgency that drove Daisy to the brink of melting with anticipation for the ultimate intimacy. Her entire body was screaming yes when he lifted himself away to tear off the rest of her clothes and shed his own.

Seeing him so highly charged with desire for her sent a burst of exhilaration through her mind. Her eyes feasted on the glitter of feverish need in his, on the powerful maleness of his perfect physique. Everything female in her quivered with delight at the prospect of possessing some, if not all of this man.

Her legs instinctively spread apart as he came back to her and exultantly wound around his hips as he plunged into where she most wanted him, deep inside, filling her with such sweet satisfaction her throat automatically emitted a soft croon of pleasure. It was so good, and unbelievably better when he began stoking the wonderful sensation with rhythmic thrusts.

She closed her eyes to everything but the inner world she was sharing with him—a world of intense feeling rolling through her in ever stronger waves. She was barely aware of goading him on with her legs, raking his back with her hands, only knowing that she wanted more and more of him, wanted him to take her to a level of ecstasy she had never known and feeling it getting closer and closer, almost unbearably close, her vaginal muscles convulsing out of all control, and she was crying out, begging…

And then it happened.

A glorious burst of release.

The torturous tension disintegrated as a sweet flood of incredible pleasure washed it away, leaving her floating in heavenly happiness with a blissful smile on her face. Ethan brushed his lips gently over hers, sharing her contentment, and she realised he had climaxed with her. Although her arms felt totally limp, she lifted them to hug him, glad that in this moment they were perfectly in tune with each other, and deeply grateful for the amazing experience he had given her. He kissed the tip of her nose, her closed eyelids, her temples, and it was so nice she couldn't stop smiling.

'You can't hide from me any more, Daisy Donahue,' he murmured in a tone of deep satisfaction. 'I was right about you all along.'

Curiosity flicked her eyes open. 'Right about what?'

He was grinning, a devilish delight dancing in his gorgeous green eyes. 'You're a challenging little witch with all the goods.'

Except the worldly goods that could make her a real match for him.

That miserably sobering thought wiped the smile off her face.

Even so she couldn't regret what she had just done with him, though the reality of her situation rushed in on her, loading her heart with a lump of anxiety. Where did *he* see them going from here? She was his employee and a very temporary one. Their positions in life were hopelessly different.

'Okay…' he drawled, placing a finger at the corner of her lips, which had lost their smile, and searching her eyes with determined purpose. 'What did I say wrong?'

'Nothing. I just remembered who you are and who I am,' she answered with black irony.

'A man and a woman who want each other.' He shook his head at her. 'Don't try to deny it, Daisy.'

She didn't. It was impossible to lie in the face of the desire that had brought them both to this bed. 'I'm not sure it's ever that simple,' she said ruefully. 'There are always…other considerations.'

'Neither of us is in a relationship. We're both adults,' he argued with arrogant confidence. 'We don't have to answer to anyone except ourselves for what we do.' He grinned again. 'And don't tell me this wasn't good. It was great! No reason not to go with it and that's what we're going to do.'

In a quick lithe movement he was off the bed and scooping her up in his arms again. 'We need a swim. Refresh ourselves,' he said, dictating action as though everything was settled between them.

She *was* hot and sweaty. A swim would be good. Maybe it would clear her head enough to think straight, which was very difficult when she was so very physically linked to him. 'You don't have to carry me.' It was a weak bid for some independence from his overwhelming attraction.

'I like carrying you.' There was a glitter of gleeful triumph in his eyes. 'I would have carried you right out of the Magic Millions marquee except you probably would have screamed abduction when you recovered from your faint. You didn't like me much then.'

The problem was she liked him too much now. In fact, she was head over heels in love with Ethan Cartwright. Was it possible that a relationship with him could have a future?

Belatedly her mind registered what he'd just told her. 'Why did you want to do that? Carry me out of the marquee, I mean.'

He laughed. 'Because you stirred the caveman in me. Still do.'

He plunged into the pool, still holding her in his arms, only releasing her underwater so she could rise to the surface as she wished. She swam away from him, needing a little time on her own to sort through the situation with Ethan. She'd thought—or had she wanted to think?—he'd given her this job out of guilt. But now it seemed he'd wanted to abduct her, keep her with him until she satisfied his caveman instincts.

He'd called her a challenging little witch.

Said he was taking *his prize*.

Was her sexual surrender simply an ego ride for him?

She swam the length of the pool several times before stopping for a breather at the shallow end. Ethan had swum beside her, apparently content to leave her alone as long as she was within easy reach, and he did instantly reach out and draw her into his embrace again, smiling into her eyes.

'The solar heating for the pool is working well,' he remarked. 'The water is at the perfect temperature for this time of day. Like warm silk. Enjoying it?'

Daisy had never been skinny-dipping before and he was right. The water was like warm silk. So was his naked flesh, seducing her into wanting more of him, despite the questions spinning around her mind.

'Yes,' she said, winding her arms around his neck, wrapping her legs around his hips. He certainly stirred the primitive woman in her—a fierce desire for total possession. Which she knew wouldn't happen, but it was so terribly tempting to have as much of him as she could.

He kissed her and she kissed him back, wishing she could lose the mountain of reservations building in her mind. His mouth broke reluctantly from hers, breathing a sigh over her sensitised lips. He lifted his hands, holding her face between them, his eyes dark green pools of desire demanding a positive response.

'I've not had nearly enough of you, Daisy. Stay the night with me. Stay the weekend.'

An iron fist squeezed her heart. How soon would *enough* come? And how much of herself would she have given him by then? Having any kind of extended affair with him could only bring her heartache and mess up her life. However wonderful this felt with him right now, it was going to be bad for her in the end. Much worse than the break-up with Carl. She shouldn't have let Ethan get to her, shouldn't let it go any further.

'I can't,' she blurted out, adding the first reason that made his invitation unacceptable. 'I live with my parents, Ethan. I'm not as free as you are. They'd worry about me.'

He frowned. 'Call them. Tell them you've been invited to have a weekend away.'

'With whom? My billionaire boss?' she mocked, the reality of the vast social gap between them finally smiting the treacherous desire he aroused in her. 'It would upset them terribly, thinking their financial problem had led me into being seduced by a man who would only be using me for his pleasure.'

He looked affronted, then fiercely belligerent. 'Don't tell me you felt no pleasure with me, Daisy. It was mutual.'

'Yes,' she readily conceded. 'And I thank you for it. But it can't go on, Ethan.'

'It's not right to let your parents rule your life,' he argued. 'You're twenty-seven, not a child.'

'They don't rule *my* life. They'd hate to even think they did. It's my decision. I care about them and I'm not going to upset them. They're going through a bad enough time as it is,' she said vehemently, gathering the strength needed to disconnect from him and make the break that a solid block of down-to-earth sanity insisted she make.

FREE Merchandise is 'in the Cards' for you!

Dear Reader,

We're giving away FREE MERCHANDISE!

Seriously, we'd like to reward you for reading this novel by giving you **FREE MERCHANDISE** worth over **$20**. And no purchase is necessary!

You see the Jack of Hearts sticker above? Paste that sticker in the box on the Free Merchandise Voucher inside. Return the Voucher promptly...and we'll send you valuable Free Merchandise!

Thanks again for reading one of our novels—and enjoy your Free Merchandise with our compliments!

Pam Powers

Pam Powers

P.S. Look inside to see what Free Merchandise is **"in the cards"** for you!

W

e'd like to send you two free books to introduce you to the Harlequin **Presents** series. These books are worth over **$10**, but they are yours to keep absolutely FREE! We'll even send you **2 wonderful surprise gifts**. You can't lose!

Chantelle Shaw
RUTHLESS RUSSIAN, LOST INNOCENCE

Kim Lawrence
MISTRESS: PREGNANT BY THE SPANISH BILLIONAIRE

Miranda Lee
A NIGHT, A SECRET... A CHILD

Carole Mortimer
THE MASTER'S MISTRESS

Trish Morey
FORBIDDEN: THE SHEIKH'S VIRGIN
Dark-Hearted Desert Men

REMEMBER: Your Free Merchandise, consisting of **2 Free Books** and **2 Free Gifts**, is worth over $20.00! No purchase is necessary, so please send for your Free Merchandise today.

Plus TWO FREE GIFTS!

We'll also send you two wonderful FREE GIFTS (worth about $10), in addition to your 2 Free Harlequin Presents books!

Order online at:
www.ReaderService.com

FREE MERCHANDISE VOUCHER

2 FREE BOOKS
and
2 FREE GIFTS

Please send my Free Merchandise, consisting of
2 Free Books and **2 Free Mystery Gifts**.
I understand that I am under no obligation to buy
anything, as explained on the back of this card.

*About how many NEW paperback fiction books
have you purchased in the past 3 months?*

❏ 0-2	❏ 3-6	❏ 7 or more
E7ZH	E7LJ	E7LU

❏ I prefer the regular-print edition   ❏ I prefer the larger-print edition
106/306 HDL   **176/376 HDL**

Please Print

FIRST NAME

LAST NAME

ADDRESS

APT.#   CITY

STATE/PROV.   ZIP/POSTAL CODE

NO PURCHASE NECESSARY!

▲ Detach card and mail today. No stamp needed. ▲

(H-P-09/10)

and used by the trademark owner and/or its licensee. Printed in the U.S.A.

▲ If offer card is missing write to: The Reader Service, P.O. Box 1867, Buffalo, NY 14240-1867 or visit www.ReaderService.com ▲

BUSINESS REPLY MAIL
FIRST-CLASS MAIL   PERMIT NO. 717   BUFFALO, NY

POSTAGE WILL BE PAID BY ADDRESSEE

THE READER SERVICE
PO BOX 1867
BUFFALO NY 14240-9952

NO POSTAGE
NECESSARY
IF MAILED
IN THE
UNITED STATES

Becoming heavily involved with Ethan Cartwright would not lead anywhere good for her. She didn't believe the Cinderella story worked in today's world. Like married like. He was only serious about getting her back into bed with him until he'd had enough of her.

She managed to summon up a crooked little smile and said, 'You won the prize. Let's leave it at that.'

Then she pushed herself away from him, resolutely determined on leaving the swimming pool, getting dressed and going home.

Tomorrow she would find another job.

Any job.

It was best if she never saw Ethan Cartwright again.

She couldn't trust herself not to give in to him if she stayed working here and putting herself in that kind of constant emotional jeopardy would be hell.

CHAPTER EIGHT

ETHAN couldn't believe it. He'd had Daisy Donahue precisely where he wanted her. She'd responded to him just as he'd imagined she would. The sex had been fantastic. Best ever. For her to reject it, reject him and all they could share together was a development he certainly hadn't anticipated. It was enough to make a man tear his hair out in frustration.

She was up the steps and out of the swimming pool before his fighting spirit erupted through the shock of being told this was all he was going to have with her. No way was he going to accept that. He'd finally found a woman who met all the criteria that satisfied what he'd always been missing and he wasn't about to let her walk away.

Which she was doing, her gorgeously perky bottom bouncing as she strode swiftly towards the cabana, stirring the caveman in him again. But this wasn't the stone age. He couldn't club her over the head and force her to stay with him. Somehow he had to challenge her decision, persuade her to change it. His mind attacked the problem from every angle as he left the pool and followed her to the cabana.

She lived with her parents.

He had to remove her from that situation so she didn't have to consider their feelings about having a connection with him, set her up independently.

But then pride came into the equation.

Her parents were unlikely to accept her rent money if she wasn't living with them and they needed it to keep the mortgage on their home running. Daisy wouldn't leave them in need.

He could pay off the lot with barely a dent in his personal wealth, free them all from the financial bind they were in, but he suspected they would take serious umbrage at such an offer. He very much doubted that Daisy's parents were people who would countenance the idea of him buying their daughter, not even to save themselves from serious debt, and Daisy herself wouldn't accept money she hadn't earned.

Money was at the heart of the barrier she was putting between them.

Because of it she was putting her own life on hold to help her parents.

But she did want him.

Impossible for her to have responded to him as she had with such passionate intensity if the attraction—the desire—didn't run deep.

Money…sex…

His mouth twisted cynically as he picked up a towel from the pile laid out on the bench beside the cabana and tucked it around his waist. He hated choosing the bartering path with Daisy but she was leaving him no other option.

A nasty thought struck.

It was quite possible that her resistance—her rejection—had actually been a ploy to force his hand, induce him to offer his expertise to fix her parents' financial problem. In fact, given the way women generally manipulated their sexual power, it was even probable.

He could do the fixing if her parents were prepared to gamble.

But he sure as hell was going to get his pound of flesh from Daisy for it!

Pumped up with ruthless purpose, Ethan entered the cabana, moved to the opened doorway to the bedroom and propped himself there, blocking the exit. Daisy had dressed so hastily there were wet patches on her T-shirt where she hadn't dried herself properly. Her body was bent over, her fingers working fast on the laces of her shoes.

'It's not so late that your parents would be worrying about you, Daisy,' he drawled. 'There's time for us to talk this situation over.'

She finished tying the laces and straightened up, her cheeks flushed, her hands clenching into determined fists at her sides, her eyes shooting unbreakable resolution at him.

'I'm grateful for the stopgap work you've given me, Ethan, but I have to move on now,' she stated, as though nothing he could say would make any difference. 'I won't come back. I'll find some other way to manage. I'm sure Charlie Hollier would keep a more frequent check on the renovations if you asked him. Please…just let me go.'

'Not until you let me have my say,' he answered, adopting a tone of reason backed by rock-like determination to win what he wanted.

One of her hands uncurled and gestured an impatient dismissal. 'It's pointless. I won't change my mind.'

'Give me the courtesy of hearing me out.'

She grimaced at the criticism of her curtness, then emitted a deep sigh of resignation. 'Say what you want to say then.'

He laid the groundwork for the barter to end up on *his* terms. 'The best estimate at the moment is five years for the market to recover. Five years for the value of your parents' investments to regain enough income for them not to need your financial input any more. Which means you'll be thirty-two before you can lead an independent life again.'

'My parents supported me for many more years than that, Ethan,' she retorted unflinchingly.

'You were a child. That was a natural responsibility. I don't believe your parents want to be dependent on you. I can't imagine they like accepting this sacrifice from you.'

She frowned. 'No, they don't like it, but the other choices...' She shook her head. 'They're not fair. They're not right.'

'I can offer a choice that will resolve the financial worry and minimise the waiting for it to be over,' he stated matter-of-factly.

She stared at him, an anguished hope in her eyes that spoke of immense inner turbulence, and Ethan instantly knew she wasn't immune to the deal he was about to put on the table. Money won. It always won if you tapped into the weakness that would give way to it.

'This will only work if you're prepared to remain on the job here in your supervisory capacity,' he ran on, blocking any escape route via some other job. 'I promise you that will be the only connection between us until after I've delivered the relief your parents need from their current debt.'

No immediate sexual pressure.

This was a waiting game.

He saw that fact register, but the money hook was in far enough for her to ask, 'How do you propose to accomplish that?'

No rush to get away from him now.

'Doing what I do—make money out of money,' he replied with sardonic satisfaction. 'When you go home this evening, tell your father I'm so pleased with how you've managed this renovations project for me, I've agreed to look at his investment portfolio and give him my expert advice on it. I'll put aside a meeting time with him at eleven o'clock on Monday morning. You have to persuade him to come.'

She nodded, looking unsure about where this was leading but willing to do anything to help her parents. 'I think he'd be quite eager to listen to your advice, Ethan.'

'I can't make him take it, Daisy, but if he does and lets me act fast enough for him, there's a very big chance his money worries will be over by the end of next month. Your parents should end up financially secure for the rest of their lives.'

'You can guarantee that?' she asked warily, not completely sold on the plan.

'No. It's a gamble, but one I'd highly recommend, not without good reason. What I can guarantee is they won't be any worse off than they are already. If your father agrees to go with my advice and it does pay off as handsomely as I anticipate, I want a reward in return.'

'You mean…a commission?'

She was shying away from where he was heading.

Maybe she hadn't deliberately set out to ensnare him into doing what she wanted of him. Irrelevant now. He wanted what *he* wanted and nothing was going to stop him from getting it. Not when she had already conceded the strength of the attraction between them by sharing that bed with him.

'No. I'd prefer your parents to think I'm doing this as a favour to you. The outcome will be you'll no longer have to give them rent money, no longer have to live with them. You can resume an independent life, free of any worry about them.' He paused to let that sink in before pointedly adding, 'And that's where my reward comes in, Daisy.'

Hot colour whooshed into her face, but there was no shock in her eyes. She had already grasped the deal he was holding out. Her expression was more a wry acceptance of his reason for making the offer. 'You want an affair with me,' she said flatly.

It vexed him that the idea of an ongoing relationship between them aroused no anticipation of any pleasure for her. Clearly she found the money angle distasteful, too. But she'd left him no other choice. He'd had to force the situation, break all the barriers she'd been putting up, clear the way.

'I'll set you up in an apartment of your own so there's no one else to consider,' he said just as flatly, still determined on the course that would give him the satisfaction she seemed intent on denying him. 'You can find another job at your leisure, carry on whatever career you set your mind to. But your free time for the rest of this year is mine.'

The rest of this year...

The time span jagged around Daisy's mind, hitting

painfully on what she had already known. Ethan Cartwright saw no real future in a relationship with her. He was proposing to keep her as his mistress, undoubtedly thinking his interest in her would lose its current edge over the months he had stipulated for exclusive rights to her free time.

'Nine or ten months on easy street should not be too big a hardship for you,' he said harshly, impatient with her silence. 'Not compared to struggling on to keep your parents out of crippling debt for five years.'

He was angry—angry that she had been bent on walking away from what they had shared in this room. The green eyes were glittering with fierce challenge. He'd probably never had his interest knocked back by a woman in his whole privileged life. And one of the reasons for that was very much on display.

Physically he was the perfect male. The towel tucked around his waist only seemed to emphasise how splendid the rest of his naked physique was, and the power of his sexuality tugged at her even now, when he was pushing a deal that made her feel like a second-class woman, only fit for his bed for as long as his desire for her lasted, tossing money at her to sweeten that humiliating truth.

But if he could do what he believed he could with her father's investments…what a huge difference it would make to the rest of her parents' lives! Instead of fretting over losing their home and moving to a much less welcoming place to the family they loved, they might even have the pleasure of helping her brothers and sister with the windfall Ethan was virtually promising.

And no one need know why it had come about.

Not the real reason.

She had to give Ethan credit for coming up with a plan to save her pride in that sense. Never mind her own personal pride. She might have to lick that wound for the rest of her life. Could she swallow the pain of being only considered mistress material for the rest of this year?

Just keep thinking of the advantages he had laid out, she savagely told herself.

They were very solid advantages. Apart from the lifting of the financial burden, there would be worry-free time for her to find her own feet again career-wise, forge a better future for herself. Besides, it certainly wasn't a hardship to have Ethan Cartwright as her lover. All she had to do was not get too tangled up emotionally with him.

'What haven't I covered?' he demanded, pushing for an answer to break the tense impasse between them, to get his teeth into whatever objection she might have.

Ethan Cartwright was a winner.

Losing was only acceptable if he'd done everything in his power to win.

Daisy couldn't help being impressed by this quality in him even as she bridled against being the target of this particular game...the prize...the reward. Those terms didn't feel special right now.

'I think you've covered everything admirably,' she said, finally making the decision to accept his proposition. 'I'll pass on your offer of advice to my father as soon as I get home.'

He nodded, a look of mocking satisfaction on his face as though he had known all along she would fall in with his plan, but would have preferred a different surrender from her. 'You have my telephone number.

Call me and let me know if he agrees to the meeting so I can rearrange my schedule.'

She nodded, wishing she had refused him, sickened by his view of her—a woman who could be bought. Not in ordinary circumstances, she thought fiercely. This wasn't primarily for herself. Her parents had always been good, hard-working people. They deserved a happy retirement. Ethan was holding out the power to give them that and she couldn't turn away from it. There were worse things than suffering the heartburn of being his mistress for the rest of this year. Much worse.

She swallowed down the surge of bile which had erupted from her churning stomach and took a deep breath. 'I'd like to leave now. If you'll move aside from the doorway…'

His eyes narrowed suspiciously. He folded his arms across his chest in a pose of deliberate rebuttal to her request. 'You haven't given me your word that we have a deal, Daisy.'

The wish to give him a bit of heartburn made her say, 'My father might not want your help. I'll let you know.'

It was a way out, free and clear of Ethan Cartwright.

He stared at her, possibly suffering a moment of uncertainty.

She savagely hoped so.

It wasn't fair that he had all the power and she had none, except for the desire she stirred in him, desire that would be thwarted if she didn't play his game. He didn't like that possibility. She could feel him seething over it and exulted in the little victory over his confidence.

The grim line of his mouth took on a sardonic twist. 'Still the challenging little witch. Well, have it your way, Daisy. The deal is on the table. Take it or leave it. I won't run after you.'

He unhitched himself from the doorway and moved aside, unfolding his arms to extend one in an invitation to take her leave.

The tension inside her was like a compressed spring, needing release. She wanted to bolt from the room. It took considerable willpower to walk at a normal pace, maintaining an air of dignity. His sexual magnetism made her insides quiver as she passed him. Her legs, however, did perform their function of holding her up and she was out of the cabana in just a few nerve-jangling moments and heading up to the house to collect her bag.

He didn't call out to her.

She didn't look back.

But she felt him watching her.

The nape of her neck tingled with heat.

Just as she reached the closest door into the house she heard the distinctive splash of someone diving into the pool. It emphatically reinforced Ethan's statement that he wouldn't run after her. She could leave his property without any fear of pursuit.

It probably should have given her a feeling of relief, but it didn't.

The plain truth was it made her feel easily dispensable from his life.

And the bitter truth was…he wasn't from hers.

CHAPTER NINE

FOR Daisy there was no escaping from the fact that if Ethan Cartwright could deliver his side of the deal, it would make a very positive difference to her entire family. Taking it meant she would have to act quickly on the offer for it to appear all above board. The most natural reaction from her was to look pleased, excited about the wonderful opportunity for her father to benefit from Ethan's financial expertise.

She worked hard at giving precisely that impression when she arrived home, bubbling over with the news that her boss would make time on Monday morning to advise her father on where he might better place his superannuation funds. The look of hope that sprang into her father's eyes relieved the tight band squeezing her heart. It was definitely worth being Ethan's mistress to lift the depression that had sapped the happiness from her parents' lives.

There was no pretence about their pleasure and excitement.

Daisy steeled herself to the sticking point and made the call.

The sound of Ethan's deep, rich voice giving his

name in response sent a shiver down her spine. The memory of how it had been in bed together was suddenly very sharp. She did want it again—wanted him. Too much. Which was where the hurt would come in. But she'd weather it somehow.

She took a deep breath and poured warmth into her voice. 'Ethan, it's Daisy. I want to thank you again for your offer, and Dad wants to thank you, too. I'm passing you over to him.'

Her father took the receiver and expressed his gratitude, as well as confirming he would keep the eleven o'clock meeting on Monday morning. Then apparently Ethan requested to speak to her again.

'Yes?' she asked somewhat breathlessly, her pulse quickening at the thought of him bringing up the relationship he expected to have with her.

'Work on the games room—the shelves and bar— begins on Monday,' he stated matter-of-factly. 'I'll be leaving early for work to make time for your father. I'll need you here to let the tradesmen in. And supervise as usual. Can I count on you?'

'Yes. No problem,' she assured him. 'I'll keep checking what they're doing against the plans Charlie Hollier drew up.'

'Fine! I'd appreciate it if you also keep leaving me your little notes at the end of each day. Progress and problems.'

'I will,' she promised.

'I'm glad you'll still be around, Daisy. I would have missed you if you weren't.'

'Well, I'm glad I rate that much,' she said dryly. 'Have a good weekend, Ethan. I guess I'll see you when I see you.'

She put the telephone down before he could say anything more personal, making it difficult to transmit to her parents that nothing out of the ordinary was going on. She knew *they* wouldn't accept the deal if they knew about it. Now that it was already in train, she had to make it work right so they would never suspect what Ethan was extracting from her as his reward.

Monday was not an easy day for Daisy at Hunters Hill. While she assiduously supervised the work being done, her mind kept fretting over what was going on between Ethan and her father at their meeting. It wasn't certain that anything would be agreed upon. Her father had always been a cautious man with money—budgeting, saving. He might find Ethan's advice too much of a gamble to take. In which case, she wouldn't have to be Ethan's mistress and there'd still be the financial problem at home.

Weirdly enough, she found herself willing the deal to go through.

And she honestly didn't know if this was because she wanted her parents to feel secure for the rest of their lives, or because she actually did want an affair with Ethan, regardless of its being a primrose path that would inevitably dwindle out. He was, without a doubt, the sexiest man she had ever met. If she could just let herself enjoy having him for the rest of this year or until he lost interest in her…surely she could manage that if she kept her head on straight about it ending sooner or later.

Her nerves were totally strung out by the time she arrived home and her mental ambivalence was finally settled by her father's announcement that he had placed his financial affairs in Ethan's hands and was convinced there would soon be an upturn in their fortunes. He wouldn't go into detail about the decisions made. Ethan had insisted on absolute confidentiality regarding the advice given. However, her father's happy demeanour clearly demonstrated he believed in it and trusted it.

The die was cast.

Now came the waiting to see if the advice proved good.

It was a strange kind of hiatus, being at Ethan's house each workday, watching it evolve into his personal home, yet not ever seeing him. He was gone before she arrived and she was gone before he returned. The only connection they had were notes they left for each other—all of them relating to the renovations.

Time rolled on. The games room with its bar was completed and the shelves were filled with an incredible array of board games, which Ethan must have had in storage somewhere. One morning she found a selection of carpet samples in various shades of green laid out in front of the staircase with a note attached—'Which one would you choose to live with?'

Why would he want her opinion?

It wasn't as if he'd invited her to live with him.

She was to be set up in an apartment, completely separate from his residence.

At first Daisy was inclined to dismiss the question, leaving a reply that read, 'It's up to you to choose.'

However, as the day wore on, she kept looking at the carpet samples, imagining how each one would look on the staircase. The moss green seemed more right than the others. Possibly she was drawn to it because it was the colour of Ethan's eyes. In the end she left a note pinned to it, saying, 'This one,' even though it was ir-relevant to her what went down in his home.

At the end of the week, the carpet-layers came in, took up the red carpet and replaced it with the moss green. It was absurd how much pleasure it gave her. Most probably her choice had coincided with his, simply reinforcing it, but she still wore a smile all day, happy that he liked what she liked. Which was true about a lot of things. And in her heart of hearts, Daisy couldn't help wishing that Ethan might come to appreciate how compatible they were and not ever lose interest in her.

Which was dangerous thinking, she sternly told herself.

Sex with her whenever he liked was Ethan's aim. It had been from the day they'd met. In one sense it was flattering that he should go to such extraordinary lengths to acquire her acquiescence to it. On the other hand, Daisy suspected it was in the nature of the man— a ruthless drive to manipulate circumstances so he would get what he wanted.

She shouldn't forget that.

The friendly little notes, the carpet question, the laying off of any physical pressure could all be a softening-up process so she would be a more amenable mistress, not a grudging one who had been pushed into the position.

The whole house gradually turned into what Ethan had envisaged. Furniture arrived—the billiard table, wonderfully comfortable sofas in moss-green velvet for the home theatre section, bedroom suites for the guest rooms. Different lighting fixtures were put in to suit the new decor, plus all the electrical apparatus for the sound system and the massive television screen.

Daisy had little left to supervise. Once the renovation of the old carriage house was done she wouldn't be needed here and still she hadn't been able to land a job elsewhere. She began to feel anxious about everything—her lack of work to justify the salary Ethan paid her, the whole money problem, whether his side of the deal would, indeed, pay off, and how soon.

Each night her father was glued to the financial report on television news programmes. Almost six weeks went by before the item he was waiting for hit the headlines. The government had approved a Chinese corporation's bid to invest in the Redback Mining Company, which was rich in iron ore deposits but too deeply in debt to exploit their holdings. The share price, which had bottomed out at five cents months ago, had already exploded up to a dollar.

Her father whooped with glee, leapt up from his armchair, pulled her mother out of hers and danced her around the lounge room in a joyful polka, yelling out, 'He did it! He did it!' in a wild version of a song from *My Fair Lady*.

He eventually calmed down enough to confide that, on Ethan's advice, he had plunged everything on the Redback Mining Company. He would sell the bulk of his shares tomorrow and make a massive profit, pay off the bank, help the family out with whatever they needed, live sweetly for ever after.

So this was it, Daisy thought, dizzied by the spectacular nature of her parents' sudden rise in fortune. Ethan had delivered. And watching her father brimming over with ebullience, her mother beside herself with happy relief and excitement, she felt a fierce gladness in the outcome of the deal, regardless of any cost to herself down the track.

Ethan was not slow in claiming his reward. The next morning a note from him spelled it out—'Make some excuse to your parents for being away this weekend and spend it here with me. I want you waiting for me when I come home after work on Friday.'

It was a straight-out demand. The first of many, Daisy realised, feeling a jolt of stark truth. Her mind had instinctively softened the situation, shaping the relationship she would have with Ethan into an affair, colouring it with hopes and wishes and desires. It struck home now that an affair was a two-way street and Ethan's mind was set on having their connection only one way—his way. That was the deal she had accepted.

The idea of being so very deeply in his power shot a shiver of fear down her spine. She was used to being her own person, making her own choices. What if Ethan's demands became intolerable? She couldn't let him completely dominate her. The line had to be drawn somewhere.

Daisy fought a sense of panic for the rest of the day, telling herself Ethan was a reasonable man. He had shown anger at what he'd considered Lynda Twiggley's tyranny. He'd treated all the tradesmen with respect. He was not about to use her badly. It wasn't in his character.

Besides, pride wouldn't allow her to show him any fear.

In fact, pride insisted she accept his demand gracefully.

In the end, she wrote him a simple little note in reply—'Thank you. I'll be here.'

Her parents were in such a euphoric state with future plans of their own, they didn't question her announcement that she would be away for the weekend, having been invited to spend it with a friend. They were eager for her to have a good time, delighted that she was free to do it and not be tight about money any more.

Daisy packed everything she thought she might need—her tennis gear, bikini, a couple of sets of casual clothes, two dressy outfits, and the gorgeous silk kimono she had bought at a second-hand designer shop, having fallen in love with the wild floral pattern that swirled with red and yellow and orange, chartreuse and olive-green.

Her mouth curled with irony as she folded this garment into her bag. It was a very apt casual robe for this weekend, since she was about to become Ethan's geisha girl. Certainly there wasn't any point in taking her pyjamas. She was careful, however, to include the contraceptive pills she'd been taking amongst the toiletries she was packing.

No way was falling pregnant part of the deal. She had her own life to live after these nine months with Ethan, establishing a new career, possibly meeting a man who would want marriage and children with her. She would only be twenty-eight when this was over.

She left home early enough on Friday morning to make a quick shopping foray at the local supermarket before continuing on to Hunters Hill. In keeping with accepting her fate gracefully and also showing gratitude for what he'd done for her parents, she'd decided to welcome Ethan home with the tastiest meal she could cook, as well as wearing her prettiest dress and looking her absolute best. Pretending it was a dinner date would surely help her feel less nervous, and hopefully stop Ethan from jumping on her bones the minute he was through the door.

It had been well over a month—almost two—since their deal had been struck, with no physical contact since then, and he wouldn't be feeling any need to carry through any seductive routine. The prize was his to take whenever he wanted. She just hoped he'd let her feel… not like a sexual commodity to be used at his convenience.

The renovations to the house had been completed so she had it to herself to do what she wanted without raising any curiosity in the tradesmen who were still fixing up the garage and the storeroom at the back of it. In between dutifully checking their progress, she cooked a lamb ragout, made the sweet corn and sour cream dip her family always devoured first at parties, wrapped slices of prosciutto ham around melon balls, opened a packet of Brie cheese and laid pitted dates beside it, prepared the snow peas and florets of broccoli for last minute microwaving.

Keeping busy helped hold the build-up of tension at bay until after the men had left for the day. Daisy then went into a frantic whirl of getting herself ready for Ethan, using one of the guest bathrooms to take a shower, wash her hair, blow-dry the long brown tresses into curling softly around her shoulders.

Her make-up took longer than usual. It was difficult to stop her trembling hands from smudging the eyeliner and making a mess with the mascara, but the end result was worth the trouble. Her eyes were her best feature and with her hair making a dark, shiny frame for her face, she looked better than Ethan had ever seen her before. Her heart was thumping with the need for him to be surprised at how attractive she could look. The hope that he might see the possibility that she could be a partner for him beyond the bedroom kept sliding through her mind, regardless of how unlikely it was.

Her dress was a lovely, feminine design, made of silk patterned in red and white swirls. It had little cap sleeves, balancing a low, sweetheart neckline which left a hint of cleavage on display. The tightly fitting bodice was styled in a crossover ruche and the swingy skirt fell in graceful folds to knee length. Her bare legs and high-heeled strappy white sandals definitely made it a sexy dress, but not overtly so. She felt good in it, and Daisy needed to feel good about herself. Especially tonight.

Nevertheless, she was hit with a painful pang of total inadequacy when she paused to examine the overall result of her efforts in the mirror. She didn't match the rich socialites Ethan was accustomed to mixing with, didn't have their sophisticated polish or their perfect styling. The woman in the mirror might have been good enough for Carl Jamieson but Ethan Cartwright was light years ahead of Carl in the eligibility stakes.

It had been stupid of her to even try to pretend this was a date. She should be wearing her usual jeans, not caring how she looked because it wouldn't change anything. For whatever reason, Ethan wanted her in his bed. She should probably greet him stark naked, save the bother of taking off her clothes, but everything within her recoiled from taking that line of brutal reality. At least making the most of herself was like putting on a brave face and she needed a brave face to cover up the nervous mess she was fast becoming.

With nothing left to do and not knowing when Ethan would arrive home, she sat in his home theatre and watched quiz shows on television, trying to keep her mind occupied by answering the questions put to the contestants.

She was ready for him.

As ready as she was ever going to be.

CHAPTER TEN

For Ethan, it had been a hectic end to the week with clients rearranging their investment portfolios after the share price for the Redback Mining Company had sky-rocketed. He was mentally fatigued by the time he finished up on Friday evening—later than he'd wanted to be with Daisy waiting for him at home. He settled into the driver's seat of his BMW and closed his eyes for a few moments, trying to re-energise himself for the night ahead—a night he'd been looking forward to, impatient for—ever since Daisy had walked away from him.

No more walking away, he thought with grim satisfaction. He didn't understand why she'd been so damned perverse about denying the natural progression of a relationship between them, but it didn't matter now. He'd won the time he wanted with her, and from her brief note, it seemed she was not about to baulk at fulfilling her end of the deal.

The power of money.

In this instance he hated it.

But he was going to take what it had bought him—take everything that Daisy Donahue could give him.

Starting tonight.

He sucked in a deep breath, rolled his shoulders, opened his eyes and began the drive home.

Over the past few weeks he'd kept up his usual social life, attending a few A-list parties, going to a couple of race meetings with Mickey, the regular games nights with the guys, holding Sunday afternoon tennis parties now that his court was ready for action. He'd actually been curious to see if any of the women he met raised a spark of interest in him—anything that might divert or supplant this obsession he had with Daisy Donahue. As absurd as it was, a businesslike little note from her gave him more of a buzz than anything else.

And despite his fatigue, he felt a buzz of anticipation growing as he drove out of the city centre, heading towards Hunters Hill. The peak-hour traffic had already thinned so the journey was not frustratingly long. It was just on six-thirty when he turned the BMW into his driveway and it gave him a sweet sense of pleasure to see Daisy's car was parked at the front steps.

She was here…waiting for him.

He drove down the side of the house to the garage, which was now in a usable state. Was Daisy listening for him to arrive? How was she feeling about losing her freedom to him? Ethan couldn't imagine her totally giving up the challenging attitude which had made winning her so compelling. The little brown sparrow had the heart of a lion.

Excitement zinged through him as he alighted from his car and strode towards the back entrance to the house. The wall of glass which gave a wide view of the harbour from the dining area and kitchen also gave a direct view inside. He halted in surprise when he caught sight of Daisy standing by the opened oven door, checking the steaming contents of a casserole dish, giving them a stir with a wooden spoon.

She was cooking him a meal?

His gaze swept the island bench. She'd laid out pre-dinner nibbles, as well. And her hair was down, falling around her shoulders in a shiny, touch-inviting curtain instead of scrunched up in a ponytail. Pleasure welled up in Ethan. He hadn't expected to be welcomed like this.

It flitted through his mind that Serena had never once cooked for him, always expecting to be taken out to restaurants or getting professional caterers in if she threw a party. Daisy wasn't in the princess mould. She hadn't put any of the tradesmen off-side with her. No getting up their noses with uppity airs and graces. She'd carried out her job here in a very diplomatic fashion.

Quite possibly cooking him dinner was a diplomatic action, as well, nothing to do with welcoming him home. Don't assume anything, Ethan cautioned himself, a wave of cynicism overriding the pleasure. She could be buttering him up to get something else from him—the good, old bartering trick. He wasn't going to fall for it. This time everything would be on his terms, exactly how he wanted it.

He resumed his approach to the back door, watching Daisy through the glass, his heart jolting again when she turned around after closing the oven door again. She looked lovely. No trace of the teenage appearance tonight. She was all woman. Some smoky make-up accentuated the bright chocolate of her beautiful eyes. Her lips were a stunning, glossy red. The upper swell of her breasts gleamed above the low neckline of her dress—a red-and-white dress—its saucy skirt swirling around her legs as she stepped quickly out from behind the island bench, her feet strapped into sexy high-heeled sandals.

She had shed the little brown sparrow image.

It had always been a deceptive image. He'd known it all along.

The lioness was out and prowling.

Desire kicked so fast into Ethan's groin, his whole body was instantly invigorated—the earlier fatigue gone and forgotten. A few quick strides and he was sliding open the glass door, enjoying the slight shock on Daisy's face as she stopped and stared at him. *Caught*, he thought, grinning with exhilarating triumph as he closed the door behind him and tossed his car keys on the dining table in passing, moving straight to the woman who could no longer escape him.

Daisy was stunned anew by Ethan's physical impact on her. Her heart started galloping. An electric tingle raced around her veins. Her stomach contracted. Weird little quivers ran down her thighs. She forgot to breathe. The welcome home speech she'd rehearsed flew right out of her mind.

He didn't give her any time to remember it. He picked her up, hoisted her over his shoulder, and was out of the kitchen and heading for the staircase before she found breath enough to speak. 'What are you doing?' she squeaked, coming out of shock enough for her dangling hands to find some purchase on his trouser belt and try pushing herself up.

'Taking you to my cave,' he replied with relish, keeping her thighs pinned to his chest with one arm and patting her bobbing derrière with his free hand. 'Did I ever tell you I loved this bottom? Sexiest bottom I've ever seen on a woman. It's been taunting me ever since we met. I think I'll eat it.'

Eat it?

'Dinner!' Daisy squawked, realising the balance of her weight made it impossible to change his hold on her. She batted *his* bottom with more vigour than he'd used on hers. 'I cooked dinner for you. It's going to spoil.'

'No. I switched off the oven. We can eat later. This hunger demands satisfaction first. Hit me some more. I like you being feisty. It's very exciting.'

She did out of sheer exasperation. 'I wanted you to appreciate my efforts.'

'I do. Red suits you. It's your true colour. Full of fire.'

'I meant the food I prepared!'

'Won't be wasted. We'll work up an appetite for it. Sex, food, wine...'

He was charging up the stairs, completely undeterred by anything she said. Part of Daisy was enraged by the indignity of being carried like a sack of grain, yet another part was excited by the rush of primitive physicality. Ethan was having his way with her and there was a kind of relief in having him act so fast. Though what was the act going to entail?

Eat her bottom?

She squirmed and thumped his some more. 'Don't think you can do anything with me, Ethan Cartwright. I won't be your sex slave.'

'You could try it,' he blithely suggested. 'You might like it.'

'I won't let you tie me up or do weird stuff like that.'

'Frightened of losing control, Daisy?'

Fear welled up in her as she recalled wondering if he was a control freak. 'You'd hate it, too,' she cried.

'Don't worry. I'm not into bondage. I want to feel your hands on me. Your hands tell me what you're feeling more eloquently than any words.'

She smacked his taut buttocks again. With relish. 'Then that should tell you I'm feeling mad at you for treating me without any respect.'

'I'm beginning to understand why men—I think it's in Finland—like having their bodies birched before sex. It sensitises the skin. Gets the blood flowing hotly.'

'Oh, you...you...'

He laughed. 'Lost for words, my sweet?'

'I'm not your sweet.'

'Oh, yes, you are! Like a very tasty lollipop. I'm going to lick you all over and make it last as long as I can. I think I'll start with your toes. They look good enough to eat. Sexy red toenails inviting me to taste them.'

Her toes curled in instinctive defence. Or was it excitement? She had terribly sensitive toes. If he started on them...

'On the other hand, maybe I want your mouth to surrender to me first,' he ran on. 'Or should I work my way up to it? Take every other bit of ground before claiming the citadel.'

'This isn't a battle,' she cried, beginning to feel frantic inside at the thought of losing all control to him and what it might mean to her. 'You've already won me, remember?'

'No. I've only won time with you. Not the same thing at all. In fact, you made me *buy* time with you. That's not a good feeling for me. I want to blot it out.'

'Being bought doesn't make me feel good either' shot straight out of her mouth.

'Got to put all that aside. Make this the real deal.'

'What deal?'

'You and me together. As we should have been.'

Her head was too dizzy to find a reply to smack his arrogant claim down, although it pounded around her mind that what was right for him wasn't right for her. They were already up the stairs and he was carrying her into the master suite and being *intimately* together was so imminent, her nervous system was going haywire and it was probably better not to think any more, to let whatever happened happen because it was unavoidable anyway.

He dumped her on the bed and followed her down, covering her body with his, lifting her hands up above her head and pinning them there as he loomed over her, a wide, wicked grin on his face. 'Forget about seizing the day,' he said. 'I'm seizing the night. You're finally mine, Daisy Donahue.'

Not *finally*.

Only for a while within the time he'd stipulated.

Until he'd had enough of her.

Unless it could somehow turn out differently.

The wish…the hope…thundered through her heart.

He lowered his head and slowly ran his tongue over her lips, making them tingle with sensitivity. 'Mmm… yummy lipstick. What's it called?'

A hysterical little laugh gurgled up from her throat. 'Passion Red.'

He grinned in devilish delight. 'Reminds me of a song in the musical *Les Misérables*. There's a line in it that goes—*"Red…the colour of desire"*. Whoever wrote it got it right.'

He kissed her with full-blooded desire, inciting Daisy to respond just as hotly. She couldn't help herself.

No matter what her head told her, her body was tuned to this man, madly eager to experience all of him again. She wanted a new deal with him, wanted the old one blotted out, wanted much more than she could ever tell him. Except with her hands.

Which he suddenly freed.

Though in a seemingly perverse action, he moved himself out of touch. His mouth broke from hers and he rolled away from her to sit on the side of the bed and lift her legs onto his lap. 'Feet first,' he muttered, working on unbuckling her sandals.

Daisy sucked in a quick breath. Her pulse was pounding through her temples. Her thighs were quivering. Her toes scrunched up in tense anticipation as he removed her sandals, stroking her ankles and the soles of her feet with tantalising gentleness. He started lifting one foot towards his mouth and Daisy tore it out of his hold and jackknifed forward, reaching out, seizing handfuls of his shirt.

'Off,' she cried in a wild frenzy—anything to avoid the toe-licking which would shoot her into uncontrollable spasms. 'Take it off so I can touch you. You said you wanted that. You said…'

'I wanted all of you,' he reminded her. 'And I do.'

It was almost a relief when he reached around her and unzipped her dress, smiling into her frantic eyes as he peeled it off her shoulders, drawing the sleeves down her arms. She hadn't worn a bra. The tightly moulded bodice hadn't required one. She felt her nipples stiffening into hard bullets as the silk fabric slid over them and fell to her waist.

'You take my shirt off, Daisy,' he commanded. 'Go ahead. Unbutton it.'

He was filling his hands with her breasts, revelling in their softness. And their hardness, his thumbs fanning the taut peaks in a slow teasing motion. Her fingers scrabbled over his shirt buttons, working as fast as they could at releasing them. She didn't linger over dragging the garment from his shoulders, wrenching it down, baring his chest, wanting them to be on equal terms, wanting it with a fierce intensity that poured from the depths of her soul.

He released her long enough to rip it off entirely and free her arms of her sleeves, as well. In a flurry of action, he scooped her into his embrace, crushing her bared breasts against the hot hard wall of his chest, pinning her there as he stood and pushed her dress and panties down over her hips and bottom.

She dug her hands between them and unzipped his trousers, hooked her thumbs on the waistband and made him as naked as she was. He lifted her chin and kissed her. She wound her arms around his neck and kissed him back, needing to lose herself in all-devouring passion. She was barely conscious of him working off his trousers, kicking off his shoes, freeing her completely of her clothes. His mouth was everywhere, her neck, her breasts, her stomach, burning trails that incited her to kiss and touch him wherever she could.

There was no more talking, only huge wells of feeling. They were back on the bed and Ethan was driving into her and her body was exploding with the sensation of having him deep inside her. They rocked together—a wild, powerful rhythm, their bodies locked in the feverish urgency to reach the ultimate peak of pleasure. Her mind swirled with the primitive triumph of possessing him as completely as he was possessing her. Her hands and legs urged him on...more, more, more...

Her inner muscles convulsed around him. He bent his head, his mouth invading hers, his tongue thrusting, reinforcing each plunge to the melting heart of her, taking an ownership that she was beyond matching, her entire body fusing as ecstatic waves washed through her, wiping out all the frenzied tension, sweeping her into a sweet nirvana made even sweeter as he climaxed and relaxed in her embrace.

It was done, she thought hazily, and there'd been no humiliation in it.

None at all.

Which made her feel a lot better about being his mistress.

Ethan hauled Daisy with him as he moved onto his side, keeping the intimate connection intact for as long as it would last. He revelled in the feeling of deep physical union with this woman, smiled ironically over the fact that she'd blown his mind again. His plan to have sex with her on his terms had been totally sabotaged. Not that he would change one bit of what they had just shared. Were still sharing, although the intensity level had eased—the lull of peace after the storm.

One thing was definitely settled. It had been well worth while helping her parents with their financial affairs. Having this with Daisy Donahue was a new benchmark in his sex life, one he couldn't imagine ever being surpassed. Of course, it could go down from here. In his experience, the highs were always at the beginning of a relationship. The best part was he'd have them all, since he had the guarantee of lots of time with her, as much time as he wanted.

He stroked her hair, content to lie quietly for a while, soak up the satisfying fact that their desire for each other *was* mutual. Not that he'd ever doubted it. Neither did he care any more why she had turned away from it before. They were together now.

A nasty little thought wormed its way into the bliss of the moment. Once the money came through for her parents and they actually had their hands on it, would Daisy still comply with the deal? What if she kissed him off and walked away, wagging her sexy bottom at him in scornful contempt for his belief in her word?

He hated being played.

And he'd hate her if she did it.

So that would be the end of any desire for her.

In the meantime, he was assured of this weekend of compliant togetherness and he'd enjoy it more if he put the trust issue out of his mind. It might not ever raise its ugly head. Daisy had a strong streak of integrity. And many other qualities he liked. He wanted to enjoy her. He *would* enjoy her.

Besides, if she did renege on the deal once his side of it had been finalised, he still came out the winner. She would have spent more time on his terms than he'd spent on her parents' financial problem.

He grinned to himself.

Before this night was out, he would definitely do everything he wanted to do with Daisy Donahue.

CHAPTER ELEVEN

THE morning after…

Daisy lay absolutely still, acutely conscious of the naked body her own naked body was intimately spooned against and the strong, masculine arm holding her there with its weight. Even asleep, Ethan was making his dominant presence felt, ensuring she remained with him in his bed.

What next? she wondered. How did he intend to fill in two whole days with her? Non-stop sex wasn't really possible, was it? Not that she had anything to complain about in that department. He had pleasured her so much and in so many different ways last night, he could go on doing it as long as he liked. Being his mistress in that sense was certainly no hardship. In fact, he was such a fantastic lover she could very well get addicted to having sex with him. Just go with the flow, and try not to get too carried away by it, she told herself. She was his toy until he got tired of her. That was the inevitable bottom line.

Probably the best attitude to adopt was to think of him as her toy, as well, not let herself take anything too seriously, enjoy everything she could while somehow building and maintaining a shield around her heart. She should try to gain some control of their relationship, at least not leave all the decisions to him.

Lying here, waiting for him to wake up and direct the play was too submissive. Surely her time was her own when he was out of action. There was no reason not to take some initiative herself, like getting out of bed and making herself coffee as she did every morning.

Very slowly and carefully she lifted Ethan's arm enough to slide out from under it. Having eased herself off the bed, she quickly headed for the guest suite where she had unpacked her bag. One look at her reflection in the mirrored doors of the built-in cupboards made an immediate visit to the bathroom mandatory. She hadn't cleaned her face of make-up last night, resulting in clownish eyes from smudged mascara, and her hair was a mess.

Daisy brushed her hair, fastened it in a top-knot, took a long, hot shower, tried not to think of Ethan's hands caressing her body as she soaped herself clean—half wondering if he would start that all over again when he did wake up—then gave herself a brisk towelling to erase the wickedly wanton tingling in her skin.

She was in the act of donning her silk kimono when the call of her name made her heart jump. Ethan's tone was not the rich, seductive purr of last night's satisfied lover. It was sharp, harsh, demanding. An apprehensive shiver ran down her spine. Was he angry at finding her gone from his bed?

Daisy's spirit of independence fiercely reasserted itself. He had not bought a slave and she wasn't going to be turned into one. She took a deep breath and stood her ground, calling back, 'I'm over here in the guest suite.'

She was tying the belt of her kimono when he barged into the bedroom, coming to an abrupt halt when he saw her. He was still stark naked and every taut muscle of his magnificent physique seemed pumped up with intimidating aggression. It was an act of will for Daisy not to freeze with fear on the spot.

The grim, fighting expression on his face slowly relaxed and the blaze of battle in his eyes dimmed as he took in the long, vivid gown she was wearing. 'The colours of Africa,' he said with a musing little smile. 'It suits you.'

Enormously relieved that the blast of tension had eased, Daisy held out her arms to show him the long drops of the sleeves. 'It's a kimono. I thought I'd be your geisha girl and make you tea.'

He threw back his head and laughed, a great peel of joyous laughter that rippled right through her heart, which should have been shielded but quite hopelessly wasn't. He strolled towards her, a huge grin on his face. 'Dinner, morning tea…you're full of surprises, Daisy. What next?'

He picked her up and twirled her around in sheer exuberance. Daisy felt like an aeroplane with her long sleeves flapping, her own spirits lifting sky-high. He was still grinning when he set her on her feet again. 'Make it coffee, not tea,' he happily instructed. 'Give me ten minutes to shower, shave and clean my teeth and I'll be down to cook you breakfast. Let me surprise you.'

He left a smile on her face—a ridiculously happy smile. She told herself it wasn't because she was stupidly in love with him. It was simply great to know he didn't expect her to be his slave. He was going to cook for her. Which probably wasn't so wonderful since he liked cooking. Nevertheless, Daisy felt much better about the situation.

Ethan was still in an ebullient mood when he breezed into the kitchen, carrying the Saturday *Morning Herald* which must have been delivered to the door. He couldn't have gone far to get it. He was only wearing the short black silk robe, which she'd found so disturbing before becoming intimately involved with the body beneath it. Daisy had no problem with looking *him* over now. It gave her a pleasurable sense of possession.

She had to remind herself he was not her man.

Ethan Cartwright was his own man.

But she didn't mind at all being his mistress when he dumped the newspaper on the kitchen bench, drew her into his embrace, cheerfully declared it was a beautiful morning and kissed her in a lovely, lingering sensual way that made her feel beautiful, even though she knew she wasn't.

'Now for breakfast!' he said, setting her aside to take command of the kitchen. 'You can sit on one of the stools on this side of the bench, drink your coffee and watch me work.'

'Okay. What are you going to surprise me with?'

The green eyes danced teasingly. 'The challenge is to serve you something that meets your *yummy* mark.'

He was yummy. As Daisy made herself comfortable on a stool, she decided to consider herself lucky to have this experience with him. The trick was in not hankering for the whole moon and stars package.

He raided the refrigerator for eggs, butter, tomatoes, bread, Spanish onions. Daisy admired his deft movements as he lined up more ingredients from the pantry…

Ethan Cartwright, very much in control of what he was doing.

Though there had been that frightening loss of cool when he'd woken up and found her gone from his bed. Had he thought she'd skipped out on the deal? He should have known she'd keep her word. Perhaps he had been scarred by other women who had taken him for a ride, using him for what he could give and not giving what he wanted back. Had something like that happened with his *ex*-fiancée—a recent serious relationship gone sour because of a lack of integrity?

He started cutting up the tomatoes and onions, shooting an oddly weighing glance at her. 'I've lined up a job interview for you if you want it, Daisy.'

A job? A real job? She hadn't managed to snag one interview for any of the positions she had applied for in the past two months. Either there were too many applications to wade through and hers was missed or her work résumé—minus her stint with Lynda Twiggley, which should have been the jewel in her crown but couldn't be mentioned due to the circumstances of her sacking—had not impressed enough.

'I'm desperate for one,' she cried. 'Please tell me about it.'

'I was chatting to one of my clients yesterday—he runs a publishing house—and he mentioned needing a good PR person for marketing, but he was dreading dealing with the response to advertising the position. Said it was a nightmare wading through the mountain of applications these days, trying to find the gold amongst the dross.'

Daisy grimaced at hearing the other side of the coin. Everything to do with the job market these days was difficult.

'So I told him about you,' Ethan ran on. 'Said you'd been behind the organisation of the Magic Millions Carnival earlier in the year. Told him I'd snaffled you to run a special project for me, coordinating and dealing with a diverse workforce, which you'd done without a hitch, and was about to move on. He more or less decided on the spot to interview you before advertising the job. You're to call him on Monday morning if you're interested.'

Just like that...on Ethan's personal recommendation, she'd zoomed straight to the top of the list. Daisy was too stunned to speak. Ethan looked enquiringly at her and she shook her head at the injustice of it all. 'It's not what you are. It's who you know,' slipped out of her mouth.

'Connections do cut through a lot of time-wasting,' he remarked. 'But this isn't a case of jobs for the boys. I'm not passing my client a lemon. I wouldn't do that. I'm confident you're capable of pulling off anything you set your mind to.'

She flushed with pleasure in his high opinion of her. 'Thank you, Ethan. And thank you for recommending me. I won't let you down.'

His mouth tilted in an ironic little smile. 'No. You're not into letting people down, are you, Daisy? Forgive me for doubting you, even for a moment.'

The moment when he'd thought she'd gone. 'You can count on me to keep my word, Ethan,' she quietly assured him.

'Yes. I believe I can,' he said, and this time his eyes twinkled with his smile. 'I'll give you all the job details after breakfast. I've written them down.'

She smiled back. 'Great! Thank you again.'

His smile stretched into a grin. 'And may I suggest

you don't wear brown to the interview. This is a guy, not a Lynda Twiggley. You'll be fronting for his publishing house. He'll want you to power-dress. Red is good. You look great in red.' His gaze dropped to her kimono. 'And orange and yellow and green.'

She laughed, a lovely bubble of joy dancing inside her. 'Okay. Not brown.' The future was definitely looking up for her, regardless of how and when this time with Ethan ended.

Breakfast was, indeed, yummy. Ethan cooked a tomato salsa with a spicy touch of Tabasco sauce, placed a poached egg in the middle of each serving and accompanied it with fingers of French toast. They shared the newspaper while they ate, which put Daisy in a very relaxed mood, no longer worrying about what they'd do for the rest of the weekend.

They played tennis. They swam and lazed around the pool. He beat her at Scrabble, right at the death, scoring eighty points with seven-letter word which Daisy declared was grossly unfair since she'd led all the way. She asked him to teach her some of the board games he played with his friends, which he willingly did. It was fun. There was not one boring or unpleasant moment, probably because underlying everything was a highly acute sexual awareness of each other, a constantly buzzing excitement that was ready and eager to burst into arousal with a touch or a kiss.

After their swim.

After Scrabble.

During the movie they semi-watched after dinner.

When they retired for the night.

Daisy did not leave Ethan's bed on Sunday morning until they left it together, satisfied that the harmony they'd reached on Saturday was still a beautiful thing between them. It continued without a hitch until after lunch, when Ethan announced he would show her the apartment she was to move into for his convenience.

He didn't use those exact words, but the illusion of mutual lovers enjoying each other was jolted straight out of Daisy's mind by the reminder of the mistress deal. The apartment *was* for his convenience—no parents to consider, no one else sharing it with her except him when he wanted to.

'Where is it?' she asked, trying to sound interested instead of totally flattened by the reality of their relationship.

'At Pyrmont. It will be handy to your work if you get the job, with the publishing house situated in Market Street—just a walk across Pyrmont Bridge to the city centre.'

Handy for him, too, dropping in after his work in the city.

She forced a smile. 'Sounds good. Let's go and see it.'

He took her to an apartment complex which had direct harbour frontage at Pyrmont. It had a community gym and indoor swimming pool for the use of all residents. They rode an elevator up to the penthouse floor and he ushered her into an apartment, which had to be worth millions of dollars with its commanding view of the harbour and the great arched bridge that crossed it.

The living area—kitchen, dining and lounge—was incredibly spacious, all making the most of the view, as did the master suite. There were two other bedrooms, a second bathroom and a study. Every room was furnished and the decor was mostly black and cream which felt very masculine. Daisy didn't see any feminine touches anywhere. Even the kitchen seemed male with its black granite benches and stainless-steel fittings.

A billionaire bachelor pad, she thought, and asked, 'Is this where you lived before moving to Hunters Hill?'

'Yes. I haven't yet decided on whether to keep it or put it on the market' was his carefree reply.

Obviously he felt no urgent need to capitalise on what had to be a huge investment.

This was how the very wealthy lived, Daisy thought as she wandered over to the wall of glass in the living room and gazed down at the white wakes of the water traffic on the bright blue harbour. She would be sharing these heights with Ethan for a while, but she had to keep remembering she was an ordinary person who would have to return to an ordinary life when his interest shifted to someone else.

This apartment probably should be delighting her. She had never had such glamorous living quarters and she would have them all to herself except when Ethan visited. Yet she could not stop a black wave of depression from rolling through her soul. Her arms instinctively folded themselves across her chest, hugging in the dark sense of misery.

Her mind insisted she should be feeling good.

Ethan had given her parents what she had wanted for them.

He was giving her a new start with the top running for a good job and a lovely place to live until she became independent again.

He was a generous man, a fantastic lover.

It was stupid, stupid, stupid, for her heart to yearn for a different situation with him. This was what she had agreed to. This was where she was, and next year she would be down there with the ordinary people. Nothing was going to change that.

Ethan had strolled on to the kitchen. He'd placed a bottle of champagne and a dish of strawberries in the refrigerator on Thursday night, planning ahead to this move with Daisy, intending to take her to bed with him after she'd looked through the apartment. As he placed two flute glasses on the bench which separated the kitchen from the dining area, he checked that she was still engaged with the view.

She'd dressed in jeans for this trip out and he smiled at the sexy way they hugged her cute derrière. This weekend with Daisy had been better than he could ever have imagined. Not only was she great in bed, she was great company, as well. He had enjoyed every minute of being with her.

He wished she was staying on at Hunters Hill. He would miss not having her there. The idea of asking her to live with him flitted through his mind, but he instantly shied away from it. Involving himself in a de facto relationship left him vulnerable to being stripped of a lot of money, possibly even losing the house he now considered his home. No way was he about to leave himself open to massive plunder.

As it was, Daisy could possibly take this apartment from him if he let her live here without paying any rent, but he'd already decided to risk that outcome. She hadn't shown any bent for filching anything that didn't belong to her and had been absolutely meticulous about not taking money she hadn't earned. Given her willingness to stick to the deal this weekend, he believed she would keep to the letter of their agreement.

Integrity was a marvellous thing.

Especially in a woman.

Of course, he could be proved wrong, but right now he had Daisy Donahue locked into a relationship with him for the foreseeable future and he saw no darkness in that future with her.

Still smiling, he loaded the bottle of champagne and glasses into an ice bucket, grabbed the dish of strawberries, and carried the lot into the master suite. He had a few more hours with her before she'd have to go home to get ready for tomorrow's interview. Ethan intended to make the most of them.

Daisy's heart jumped at Ethan's touch as he slid his arms around her waist. She hadn't heard him come up behind her, the thick cream carpet muffling any sound of footsteps. He gently pulled her back against him, bending his head to brush her hair away from her ear with his cheek. 'Happy with the view?' he murmured, his warm breath tingling over her skin.

'Yes. Who wouldn't be?' she answered, making a conscious effort to relax and be happy with what she did have of him.

'You could move in tomorrow afternoon.'

So as to be ready for him tomorrow night...his convenient mistress.

Daisy clamped down on the bitter thought. She had nothing to be bitter about. Nothing!

'I should be able to do that,' she agreed. 'I'll have to square it with my parents first.'

'Say the friend you spent the weekend with has asked you to share an apartment in the city. It's the truth.'

True enough, she thought, and the move made sense

if she was offered the job at the publishing house. Her parents wouldn't quibble over it. They were happy, making plans for their future, and would be happy for her to do whatever she wanted.

And she wanted him.

There was no denying that truth.

She wanted him for as long as she could have him.

On a fierce wave of determination and desire, Daisy wheeled around in his embrace, flung her arms around his neck, and kissed him in a savage need to put everything else aside, to generate once again the intense, all-consuming passion where nothing else mattered.

Seize the day…

She would face whatever tomorrow brought when tomorrow came.

CHAPTER TWELVE

TO DAISY'S astonishment, delight and immense relief, she was given the PR job at the end of the interview—no waiting to hear and no waiting to start work, either. Her new boss remarked that since Ethan Cartwright was prepared to release her from his project and he, himself, needed her services immediately to set up a publicity tour for a new author, he'd like her to begin tomorrow. Even better, the salary being offered was more than she had ever earned before.

It made her wonder if Ethan had exaggerated her worth. Certainly his personal recommendation had worked wonders. Of course, it all fitted nicely into his plan for her to move into his apartment today, but it would suit her, too, which was readily understandable to her parents—a simple case of picking up her independent life again since their financial problems had been resolved. She had already told them she'd seen an affordable place at Pyrmont at the weekend and intended to take it.

It was up to her now to make a success of this new career, get it solidly established so there wouldn't be too big a hole in her world when her time with Ethan was over. Ever since she had lost her job with Lynda Twiggley, she had been inescapably dependent on him. The apartment was part of the deal, but at least he was no longer the only source of income for her. She would be able to strike out on her own whenever she had to. That was a good feeling.

There was more champagne that night to celebrate the beginning of her new career. Ethan was happy for her to be happy about it. Certainly he saw it as no threat to what he wanted with her. Even when she explained that a publicity tour would involve overnight trips to Melbourne and possibly other capital cities, he made no objection, seemingly taking it for granted she would not always be free when he was free.

He was definitely not a control freak.

And Daisy was hopelessly in love with him.

She looked forward to the evenings he spent with her during the week. Never on a Tuesday night because that was games night with his old friends, but most other days he dropped in at the apartment after work. They chatted over a relaxing drink, cooked dinner together, watched television, made love, after which he would always go home.

It made her wonder if that was some legal point with him—protection against any claim she might make on him in court when he wanted out of their relationship. She was living in his apartment, but they were not live-in lovers. They weren't a couple in public, either. Although he invited her to Hunters Hill on weekends, it was only ever the two of them there—no parties. He didn't take her out nor ask her to accompany him to any social events. Which all hammered home to Daisy that she was his private mistress and for anything more to develop between them was sheer pie in the sky.

Having resigned herself to taking each day as it came, she could hardly believe it when Ethan suddenly changed the parameters of their relationship. They were lying in bed one Sunday morning, languorously content not to move for a while.

'It's the Golden Slipper next Saturday,' he remarked, running gentle knuckles up and down the curve of her spine.

'What's the Golden Slipper?' she mumbled, nestling her head under his chin.

'Only the richest horse-race for two-year-olds in the world,' he answered dryly. 'The prize money is two million dollars and Mickey has Midas Magic lined up to win it.'

Ethan's horse—the one that had won the Magic Millions just before the terrible debacle with Lynda Twiggley, which had been immediately followed by Ethan's determined drive to have her in his life. 'I guess you want to go and see him race,' she said, thinking of spending the day shopping since he wouldn't want her with him in some celebrity marquee where his high-society friends would be gathered.

'I know you're not into gambling, Daisy, but I think you'd find it a fun day anyway. Fashions in the Field can be eye-popping stuff. There's the whole glamorous spectacle of the Golden Slipper ceremony, plus live entertainment—a guest star singing. Mickey has booked a table for ten in the Winning Post restaurant which has the best view of all the action. We can sit there, eating a gourmet lunch, drinking fine wines and watching it all unfold below us.'

Daisy could hardly believe her ears. She jerked up to look him in the eye. 'You want me to go with you? Be introduced to your friends?'

He frowned at her incredulous tone. 'They won't be all strangers to you. You saw Mickey at the Magic Millions and you know Charlie.'

'Yes, but I thought…' She struggled to find the right words. 'I thought you were keeping me in the background of your life. Not upfront.'

His frown deepened. 'You were worried about what your parents might think of our connection. I was waiting for a reasonable amount of time to pass in your current career for them to accept it was okay for me to pursue my personal interest in you.' He grimaced. 'There's bound to be publicity about us once we're seen together.'

Daisy was stunned again. She'd had it all wrong. Totally wrong! He'd been considering her, caring about her. In one huge galloping leap, the hope she had so sternly repressed emerged from its dark dungeon and bloomed in bright sunshine. She had just been elevated from secret mistress to public partner. Her heart skipped and jumped in wild joy. There was a chance this relationship could become a serious one if Ethan was happy for them to be seen as a couple.

'I have to go shopping. Today,' she announced, giving him a look of determined purpose. 'I won't have enough free time during the week to find something suitable, Ethan.'

'You could wear your red-and-white dress,' he suggested. 'You look great in that.'

'No, it won't do.' She shook her head emphatically. 'I saw what your crowd wore at the Magic Millions, remember? I need a fantastic outfit with a matching hat.' She grinned at him. 'Not brown.'

He laughed. 'Okay. I'll take you shopping, buy you whatever you want.'

'No, you won't!' she cried indignantly, bridling against being put in the bought mistress bracket again. 'I have to accept the free accommodation you give me because of the deal I agreed to, but I'm making good money now and I can afford to buy some fine feathers of my own, thank you.'

She flounced off the bed and stood up in a challenging stance, hands on hips. 'Those are *my* terms, Ethan.'

He rolled onto his side, propping himself up on his elbow, the green eyes regarding her with a glint of triumph, as though he had just won something. 'Then I'll just tag along, be your chauffeur, take you to lunch somewhere along the way.'

She couldn't argue with that. Her free time was exclusively his. Besides, having lunch with her out in public was more delightful proof that he didn't want her kept hidden away. Nevertheless… 'I'd prefer you not to be with me in the boutiques. It's much more fun for me to surprise you on the day.'

He smiled. 'I'll park myself in a coffee shop with the Sunday newspapers.'

Daisy smiled back, bubbling with joy inside. 'You'd better come and shower with me. We have to get moving. And I warn you this might be a marathon shopping trip. I'm not going to settle for anything less than spectacular.'

Pride insisted she look at least as good as anyone in his party—good enough to be accepted as Ethan's partner in everyone else's eyes. She wanted to make him feel proud to have her on his arm, make him feel she could be his partner in every sense. For the first time she thought it could be a real possibility. It wasn't about just having her in his bed. It was about pursuing his interest in her.

Ethan felt an exhilarating sense of triumphant satisfaction all week, leading up to the Golden Slipper Saturday. Daisy's response to being with him for the big horse-race proved beyond a doubt that his judgement of her character had not been astray. If she'd been into bartering sex for gain, she would have pounced on his offer to buy her clothes. And he was quite sure now she would walk out of his apartment at the end of the year—the deal done—without any thought of making a claim on it.

His cynical view of her resistance to having an affair with him—a form of manipulation to get him to solve her problems—no longer seemed feasible. There was nothing underhand about Daisy. She played everything straight down the line. Best of all, since the way had been cleared for her to have an open relationship with him, she seemed happy about it. Genuinely happy. Which meant he wasn't buying her submission to what he wanted of her any more.

He was tempted to remove all force from the situation, free her from the deal, but he liked having her in his apartment, liked having the security of knowing she was his to have. As it stood, she couldn't walk away from him, not without breaking her word, and Daisy wouldn't do that. He wanted more time with her. It was stupid to risk not having it.

Mickey called him at work on Friday. 'Just letting

you know Midas Magic had a great trial run on the track this morning,' he said, his voice brimming with cheerful confidence. 'And in case you're not already aware, Serena has attached herself to James Ellicott.'

James Ellicott... Ethan winced at one of his clients being sucked in by Serena. The man had made a fortune in advertising and had already been divorced twice, costing him a lot of money in settlements. He liked beautiful women and was apparently prepared to pay for them.

'They were both here at dawn watching his horse trial,' Mickey ran on. 'No doubt she'll be included in his party dining in the Winning Post restaurant tomorrow. Thought I'd better warn you.'

'Thanks, Mickey. No problem. I'm not the least bit troubled about Serena being with someone else.'

It was true. Though Mickey's news report had instantly incited the cynical thought that Serena was buttering up another billionaire for the kill. She was not a morning person. If James Ellicott married her, she wouldn't be accompanying him to dawn trials again. He would have to be satisfied with her gracing his arm in the winners' circle, which Serena would do beautifully.

Ethan suddenly realised that should Midas Magic win tomorrow, he and Daisy would be in the spotlight for the presentation of the Golden Slipper. She'd been delighted with her shopping trip. He hoped her outfit was spectacular enough to shut Serena's mouth because his ex-fiancée had no grace at all when it came to losing.

When he walked into the apartment the next morning, any worry that Daisy might be put down by *anyone* disappeared in a flash. She looked absolutely gorgeous. And elegant. And so sexy, desire instantly sizzled through him, making his tailor-made suit feel more snug than it should around the groin area.

Impossible to race her off to bed. It would mess up the image she had created and it was too marvellous to spoil. She twirled around in front of him, the calf-length skirt swirling in a froth of vivid colour. 'Like it?' she asked, her big chocolate-brown eyes sparkling with confidence in her fine feathers. 'It's called *neon butterfly.*'

The dress was a brilliant pink, the shiny silk patterned with white and purple and orange and bright green butterflies. Its low V neckline and the wide band from under her breasts to her waist emphasised her beautiful, womanly curves. Her long, dark brown hair was piled on top of her head, and curling from one ear over her crown was a stunning concoction of bright pink flowers and feathers.

'I'm dazzled,' he said, shaking his head in bemused appreciation. Gone was the brown sparrow. This butterfly would outshine every other woman at the Rosehill Gardens racetrack.

Her smile wavered. A flash of wary vulnerability took the sparkle from her eyes. 'Is that good or bad?'

He grinned, warmly assuring her, 'It's amazingly good,' as he walked forward to draw her into his embrace. 'I'll have to beat off Mickey from trying to steal you from me, because he'll definitely see you as the most beautiful fish in the sea today.'

She laughed, relief melting into pleasure. 'I just didn't want to let you down, Ethan.'

'You never let me down.' He kissed her forehead and smiled into her eyes. 'And that's something I really value, Daisy.'

'You haven't let me down, either,' she rushed out somewhat breathlessly, and there was a yearning look in her eyes—a look that did something weird to Ethan's heart. It was as if a hammer had smashed into the hard shell he'd kept around it since his disillusionment with Serena, and a gush of warmth made his chest swell with waves of emotion.

He wanted to look after this woman.

Protect her.

Give her everything she needed.

The instincts that had driven him to act as he had when he had first met her suddenly made perfect sense. The need to have her, to nail her into a relationship with him…it was because she was uniquely special in his experience…a woman he could trust, a woman he could love, a woman he could share his life with.

The look in her eyes told him she wanted to be convinced that could happen and the realisation hit him that all along she hadn't believed it was a possibility. Her determined avoidance, her resistance to an affair with him, her stunned surprise that he wanted her to appear in public with him…she simply hadn't believed a relationship with him would work, that it would always be limited to sex on his terms.

And that wasn't good enough for Daisy Donahue.

Nor should it be.

Today was a testing ground.

He must not let her down.

CHAPTER THIRTEEN

Daisy and Ethan arrived at Rosehill Gardens in a chauffeured limousine—no parking problem, no drunk-driving problem. A crowd of people were milling around the entrance gates, waiting to get in, although showing no impatience about it. It was a bright sunny day and everyone seemed to be in a festive mood—the men mostly dressed in suits, the women favouring cocktail dresses, with more of them wearing fascinators than hats, which gave Daisy extra assurance that her outfit had been a really good choice.

As Ethan escorted her towards a side gate with his member's pass in hand—no queuing for him—quite a few people turned to look at them. Ethan, of course, was a strikingly handsome man, superbly attired in his grey pin-stripe suit, white shirt and gold and grey silk tie, but Daisy felt she really matched him today, as well as she could.

'Hey, Daisy!'

The call of her name startled her and she stopped dead as she spotted Carl Jamieson striding out from a group of people, grinning at her as though he was delighted to claim acquaintance with her again. With unbelievably crass arrogance he ignored the fact she was with another man and focussed entirely on her.

Still grinning, he said, 'You look fabulous, Daisy. No more penny-pinching, huh?'

Daisy instantly stiffened with resentment. Her ex-boyfriend was proving once again he was a fine weather friend. 'I didn't know you were into horse-racing, Carl,' she said coldly.

'It's not usually my bag. I'm here with a bachelor party. One of the guys is getting married tomorrow.'

'Then I suggest you rejoin your party.'

His ego took umbrage at her blanket rejection and he shot a sneering look at Ethan. 'Got better fish to fry, have you?'

'Yes, she has,' Ethan replied with unruffled aplomb. 'And I suggest you take Daisy's advice and return to your party.'

Carl's chin jutted up belligerently, but something in Ethan's expression quickly changed his mind about challenging anything. 'Fine!' he snapped. 'Have fun!'

Ethan's arm tightened around hers as Carl turned his back on them. 'Let's move on,' he murmured.

Daisy forced her feet to fall into step with him. 'Sorry about that,' she mumbled. 'I didn't expect to run into him here.'

'Your ex-boyfriend?'

She winced. 'Yes.'

'I'm glad you didn't give him any encouragement,' he said dryly.

She lifted her gaze to his and found amusement twinkling in his green eyes. Her vexation with Carl broke into a giggle. 'Well, he was very rude, Ethan, breaking in on us like that.'

He smiled with devilish humour. 'And got his just deserts.'

Having regained her pleasure in the day, Daisy hugged his arm as they moved past the gate and strolled up the rose-bordered path to the pavilions overlooking the racetrack. She sniffed the scented air and felt a blissful joy in Ethan's company. He was so different from Carl—caring, considerate and best of all, a giving person. Although he did want what he wanted in return. Which was fair enough, Daisy decided.

He had also stood up to Lynda Twiggley on her behalf—not that she had appreciated it at the time—and she had no doubt he would have dealt comprehensively with Carl's rudeness if her ex-boyfriend had pushed it any further. He was definitely the kind of man she wanted at her side. If only it could last...

'I should probably mention that my ex-fiancée will be here today, too,' he suddenly drawled.

All the lovely warmth she had been feeling was plunged into ice.

He had never spoken of his ex-fiancée.

Daisy only knew of her through Charlie Hollier.

Was this why Ethan had invited her to the Golden Slipper, to show his former love he was happily involved with another woman? Off with the old, on with the new?

'I broke up with her last year,' he said matter-of-factly. 'I wouldn't put it past her to be rude to you on the sly. If that happens, Daisy, it's because she didn't get what she wanted. Okay?'

She glanced up at him, needing more information than that to ease her inner tension. 'Why did you break up with her?'

His mouth took on a cynical twist. 'I found out the money was more important than the man to her. She's with James Ellicott now. I don't think he cares why as long as he has her.'

She knew of James Ellicott. The flamboyant billionaire was quite ugly compared to Ethan, his big physique made bigger by a beer belly, his sandy hair thinning on top and a large nose dominating his face. Regardless of his looks, he had acquired a beauty queen and a famous model as wives in the past.

'Is your ex-fiancée very beautiful?' she asked.

'On the outside, yes. And she knows how to trade it. I was completely fooled for a while. I'm glad the wool was pulled off my eyes before I married her. Believe me, that relationship is stone-cold as far as I'm concerned.'

What she had with Ethan was still running hot, but... 'I traded myself for money, too,' she blurted out, all her insides squirming horribly at that undeniable truth. She had no chance of a really solid relationship with Ethan. None at all.

He halted, turning to her, gently cupping her cheek and chin with his free hand, his gaze burning into hers with absolute conviction. 'Not for yourself, Daisy,' he said quietly. 'Your character is so far removed from Serena's, it's like night and day.' He lightly pinched her cheek and smiled. 'Now smile back at me because we're going to have a happy day together.'

She did smile back, intensely relieved that he didn't see her as similar to Serena, despite their deal, which was still in force. It actually seemed he was dismissing it as of no account at all.

'That's my girl,' he said warmly, and the possessive note in his voice sent hope soaring through her heart again, making Daisy determined to be happy, no matter what happened throughout the course of the day.

Ethan gave her a tour of the amenities provided for race-goers at Rosehill Gardens—every taste and class-level catered for. There was a buzz of excitement every-where, people partying, having fun. Some groups were wearing mad clothes and hats, adding to the colour of the scene. Many of the young women were wearing in-credibly high-heeled shoes and Daisy wondered how their feet would fare by the end of the day. She was glad that her strappy gold sandals were not so high and easily walkable in because they were doing a lot of walking.

Eventually they met up with Ethan's friends in the Champagne Bar. Charlie Hollier did a double-take when he saw her. 'Wow, Daisy! That's some transformation!'

She laughed. 'Well, I couldn't come to the Golden Slipper in jeans, Charlie.'

'Oh, I don't know,' Ethan drawled. 'You always looked sensational in jeans, too.'

'Okay, you guys,' one of the women chided good-humouredly. 'You can stop drooling and start introductions.'

Daisy, glowing from the compliments from both men, did her best to memorise the new names. Mickey Bourke fetched glasses of champagne for them and it was his girlfriend, Olivia, who raised the background question, her curiosity piqued by the men's comments.

'So where are you from, Daisy, and how did you and Ethan meet?'

'I can tell you that,' Mickey cut in archly. 'Daisy was doing PR at the Magic Millions back in January and Ethan was so taken by her he almost carried her off. Had to stop him from making a fool of himself.'

'January!' one of the other women, Allyson, exclaimed. 'But we haven't seen Ethan with Daisy until now!'

'Most difficult woman I've ever met,' Ethan rolled out in a tone of mock exasperation. 'First up she didn't like me. Didn't want anything to do with me. On top of that, I interfered between her and her boss and caused her to lose her job, which made me not only unlikeable but a total villain, as well.'

He threw up his hands and they all laughed at Ethan Cartwright in such a dilemma.

'So then I had to turn myself into a hero and give her a job until she found another suitable PR position,' he continued.

'Supervising the renovations of his house,' Charlie chimed in. 'And let me tell you she was a stickler for detail. Didn't let the tradesmen slip up on anything. They didn't need any supervision from me until after Daisy left.'

'But did she look kindly on me for this rescue act?' Ethan queried theatrically. 'As far as Daisy was concerned I was just another boss. I remember very clearly her first day at the house when I was doing my best to charm her. She looked sternly at me and laid down the law—*the master of the house does not dance with the staff.*' He rolled his eyes and pulled a sad grimace. 'No dancing with Daisy.'

Everyone was vastly amused by his show of frustration.

'This has to be a first for you, Ethan, having your interest in a woman turned down,' one of his old friends from Riverview, Dave Marriot, commented, grinning widely. 'Now you know what it's like not to be an instant winner.'

'And good for you, Daisy, keeping him on toast,' his wife, Shannon, said approvingly. 'Guys like Ethan get used to women falling in their laps.'

'I didn't deliberately keep him on toast,' Daisy quickly slid in. 'It just took me a while to realise he wasn't so insufferably arrogant, not caring about anything but what he wanted.' She smiled up at him. 'I found myself liking him for lots of reasons. He didn't even mind when I was beating him at tennis.'

'You beat Ethan at tennis?' Mickey crowed.

She laughed. 'No, he won in the end. He made the mistake of going easy on me early on and the set went to a tie-breaker.'

'I give you all fair warning,' Ethan said. 'The next tennis party I hold, Daisy and I are going to wipe everyone else off the court.'

'Was that how you finally won her over, being a good sport?' Olivia asked, looking thoroughly entertained by the story.

'No. I was still the boss and Daisy has principles with a capital *P*.' He sighed over her recalcitrant attitude, making everyone laugh again before he delivered the punchline. 'I had to wait until she moved on to a new PR position at a publishing house. Only then did she consider it appropriate to let me into her personal life. Which is why you haven't seen her with me before today.' He tossed off a helpless gesture. 'All her doing, not mine. As I said, a terribly difficult woman.'

It was a very clever spin on the real story and Daisy was deeply grateful that it made their relationship so readily acceptable by his friends. Who she was didn't matter. They simply loved the idea of Ethan having to chase her for months to win what he wanted, which clearly made her quite marvellous in their eyes.

And made Ethan even more marvellous in hers.

There'd been no ego in that story. He had deliberately played her up and played himself down and she loved him all the more for it. The tension she'd been feeling about meeting his friends had been completely dissipated, and the foundation set for a delightfully happy day together.

They moved on to the Winning Post restaurant, the starched white linen tablecloths and classy settings adding their special touches to it. The floor was constructed in tiers, giving all the diners, wherever they sat, a clear view of the action out at the racetrack. For an even closer look at every entire race, a television set was attached to each table.

Directly below them was the parade ring where the horses circled around before moving out to the starting gates. At one end of that was the stage where presentations of prizes were made and other entertainment took place. Just beyond this area was the finishing line for each race. All the fences were lined with roses in full bloom. It was a great view with much to see and enjoy.

They had just sat down when they saw a helicopter coming in to land in the middle of the field. 'James Ellicott making his usual entrance,' Mickey remarked, shooting a quizzical look at Ethan who shrugged and openly said, 'No problem. Daisy knows about Serena.'

'And may I say I much prefer your current partner,' Charlie said, grinning at Daisy. 'I'm far more comfortable with down-to-earth than airs and graces any day.'

'Yes, Serena does tend to put it on,' Allyson commented with a warning look. 'Don't let her patronise you if she stops at this table to say hello.'

'Just remember, you've got Ethan. She hasn't,' David pointed out.

'And I bet James Ellicott is second prize in her book, so watch out, Daisy. Serena can be a bitch when she doesn't get her own way,' Shannon put in.

It amazed and warmed her that they were all on her side. While it might be out of loyalty to and support for Ethan, they did seem to genuinely like her.

The first course of their gourmet lunch was served, a delicious chicken and pistachio nut terrine, accompanied by a glass of a very good Chardonnay. Daisy relaxed and enjoyed herself. The mood of the party was highly convivial and Ethan was looking after her as though she really was a prize he'd won.

They had just started their entrée—a smoked salmon parcel containing crab and avocado and tomato—when James Ellicott led his party into the restaurant, making a somewhat boisterous entrance. He descended on their table, loudly but good-humouredly declaring, 'I see the opposition is here already. Got to say Mickey's got Midas Magic running well, Ethan, but I'm betting on my horse for The Slipper.'

'Each to their own, James,' Ethan answered equably, standing up to shake hands with the man, who had a stunningly beautiful blonde in tow—skin like porcelain, cornflower blue eyes, an hour-glass figure poured into a high-fashion black-and-white suit with a matching hat that only an amazingly creative milliner could have made.

'Who's your little filly?' the big man demanded, eyeing Daisy with interest. 'Haven't seen her around before.'

'Daisy, may I introduce James Ellicott and Serena Gordon. Daisy Donahue.'

'What a quaint name!' Serena drawled, icy blue eyes sizing Daisy up as she stood to acknowledge the introductions.

'I think it's a great name, full of sparkly sunshine,' Ethan quickly slid in, smiling his approval of it.

It probably stopped his ex-fiancée from saying it was usually attached to a cow.

'Hello to both of you,' Daisy said brightly, shaking James's offered hand.

'A pleasure to meet you, Daisy Donahue,' he replied, as though relishing the roll of her name off his tongue, twinkling hazel eyes flirting with her. The man was definitely a womaniser with a big personality to go with his even bigger pockets.

'I see you're wearing Liz Davenport,' Serena remarked, naming the designer who'd created *neon butterfly*.

'Yes,' Daisy answered in surprise, not being so familiar with the fashion scene that she could actually recognise individual styles.

'She seems to have gone all gaudy this year.'

Daisy smiled to take the sting out of the snipe. 'I guess, with your colouring, you don't wear bright colours well.'

'Each to their own,' she said, giving Ethan a mocking look as she parroted his words. 'I much prefer European designers. James bought this Christian Dior suit for me in Paris.'

'How lovely for you!' Daisy said sweetly. 'I hope your outfit gives you as much pleasure wearing it as I'm having wearing mine.'

She sniffed haughtily and patted James's arm. 'Let's move on to our table, darling. I'm dying of hunger.'

'Got to feed the beauty and the beast,' he said jokingly, grinning at Ethan. 'Good luck with Midas Magic!'

'Good luck with your choice, too,' Ethan replied.

They moved on.

As she and Ethan resumed their seats at the table, Shannon raised a hand and said admiringly, 'Daisy, I salute you. That was a brilliant piece of sticking it right back at Serena.'

'Believe me, give Daisy a challenge and she rises to it every time,' Ethan declared, making them all laugh again at how challenging she had been to him.

Daisy was awash with pleasure. Ethan was proud of her. And he'd said so many complimentary things about her, leaving his friends in no doubt he held her in high regard, she was beginning to believe anything was possible between them, no limits at all on their relationship.

The races were watched and commented upon between the many courses of their lunch. Mickey had to leave the party when two other horses he'd trained were running. He returned each time in a celebratory mood after the horses had performed well, one coming second, the other third.

'Waiting for the big one,' he told Ethan with ebullient confidence.

The big one was preceded by an amazing ceremony. A helicopter hovered over the field beyond the finishing line as a man carrying a box descended on a rope to a podium which had been set up over there. A string of models wearing gold catsuits moved out across the racetrack, forming a line between the podium and the stage in the parade ring. The man unlocked the box to reveal what actually was a golden slipper. He presented it to the model closest to him, who passed it to the next, and so on down the line to the stage while an operatic tenor sang 'Nessun dorma'.

'Time for us to go,' Ethan said, taking Daisy's hand as he rose from his chair.

'Go where?' she asked. Mickey had already left the table to ensure everything was right for Midas Magic.

'To one of the owner's boxes beside the stage. We have to be on hand for the presentation if Midas Magic wins.'

As she leapt up to accompany him she saw that James Ellicott and Serena Gordon had already vacated their table. It only took a few minutes via a long elevator to arrive at the parade ring. The master of ceremonies was still introducing the jockeys who were to ride and photographers were everywhere, taking shots of the scene. A formal usher opened the gate for Ethan and Daisy to enter the fenced-off area and Ethan escorted her to the only empty box left—the rest of them already occupied by groups of people.

'Most of the horses are owned by syndicates,' Ethan explained. 'Mickey talked me into buying Midas Magic outright so we're on our own here, Daisy.'

Together, she thought happily.

They didn't have long to wait for the big race. They watched it on the huge television screen set up for the crowd and Daisy found herself sharing Ethan's excitement as Midas Magic shot to the front at the turn and sped away from the rest of the field, winning by seven lengths as though he was in a league of his own.

'What did you feed that horse, Ethan?' James Ellicott yelled out from his box.

'It's all in his genes,' he yelled back. 'You should listen to Mickey about bloodlines, James.'

Daisy couldn't help grinning at the vexed look on Serena Gordon's face. She felt like a huge winner today.

Ethan took her up on the stage with him for the presentation. He made a charming speech, giving all credit to his friend for the win, calling Mickey a brilliant trainer, then smiling at Daisy while saying Midas Magic had brought some magic into his life and he hoped it would last for a long, long time.

Some magic…her?

Daisy tried to caution herself not to read too much into everything Ethan said today. She was riding such a dizzying high, it was difficult to grasp any down-to-earth common sense. Nevertheless, she did manage to remind herself that when Ethan set out to do something, he carried it through, covering every detail. He was determined on having a happy day which meant giving her one, too. Midas Magic winning was icing on the cake— two million dollars' worth of icing! He was probably so happy, wonderful words were simply spilling off his tongue.

And continued to do so.

On their way back to their party in the Winning Post, they were accosted by Lynda Twiggley. 'Ethan!' she cried, pouncing on his arm, her eyes glittering with gambling triumph. 'What a fabulous win! Congratulations! I bet on Midas Magic again.'

'Splendid!' he tossed at her.

She gave Daisy a saccharine smile. 'And *you've* certainly come up in the world, Dee-Dee.'

Ethan pointedly picked her hand off his arm, saying in a cutting tone, 'Ms Twiggley, my partner's name is Daisy Donahue, who, I might add, is well worth knowing. A loss to you. A win to me. Have a good day!'

He swept Daisy off, leaving Lynda Twiggley's mouth agape. It was marvellous! Bubbles of joy inside Daisy burst into giggles as they rode the elevator up to the restaurant.

'What?' Ethan asked.

She sucked in a sobering breath, but her eyes were still dancing with laughter as she looked up at him. 'I did hate being called Dee-Dee.'

'Insufferable woman! I hated how she treated you. I was right to rescue you from her, Daisy.'

'Yes, you were,' she had to agree. Despite all her heartache over the past few months, she was in a far better position at the publishing house and whatever happened with Ethan, she was happy to have had him in her life.

Ethan felt intensely gratified by this admission from Daisy. She had been at war with him for so long, holding out against his siege, only giving in under force. To have her freely concede that he had been right to push for where they were now really did make him a winner.

There was not the slightest bit of tension coming from her for the rest of the day. She was completely relaxed with his friends, showed open affection towards him, delighted him with her attitude towards everything, and incited a burning build-up of desire which took all his willpower to keep under restraint until he had her to himself again.

The moment the door of the apartment was closed behind them, she was in his embrace and kissing him back as feverishly as he kissed her. They were on fire together, couldn't have enough of each other, and she discarded her clothes as urgently as he discarded his, leaping onto the bed, welcoming him with open arms, her legs winding around him in fierce possession. The sex was fast and incredibly intense, mounting swiftly to an explosive climax that was totally out of his control but he didn't care. She shared it with him and she was all his…all his…

Until the telephone rang.

CHAPTER FOURTEEN

DAISY automatically reached out and picked up the telephone receiver from the bedside table, not even wondering who was calling, her mind still floating from the pleasure of the deeply intimate connection with Ethan. It was a jolt to hear her mother's voice.

'Oh, good! You're home! I thought you might still be out partying.'

'Partying?' Daisy repeated, trying to get her wits together. She sat bolt upright and shot Ethan a warning look, putting a silencing finger on her lips.

'We saw you on television, standing right next to Ethan Cartwright when he was presented with the Golden Slipper. It was such a surprise. We couldn't believe our eyes. You didn't tell us you were going out with him.'

The chiding tone caused Daisy's heart to skitter all around her chest. She took a deep breath to shoot some oxygen into her brain, knowing she needed an explanation that sounded reasonable. 'Well, Mum, it was our first date and I didn't know what to expect. I wasn't sure. I mean he's such a high-powered person, I felt nervous about going out with him, fitting in with his friends. It might have ended up awful, so I didn't want to tell you about it. But I actually had a wonderful time. It was a marvellous day.'

'Your first date.' Her mother sounded pleased. 'You looked beautiful, dear. Such a gorgeous dress and head-piece. Did you buy it especially?'

'Yes. I splurged, but the outfit made me feel good so it was well worth the money. Lucky I have such a highly paid job now.'

'And it's lovely that you're spending your money on yourself instead of on us.'

'I didn't mind that, Mum.'

'Well, thank heaven it's behind us. Or I should say thank Ethan Cartwright for his good advice. When we saw you together on the television, your father wasn't as surprised as I was. He thought the man must have been sweet on you all along to have offered his help with our financial problems. Will you be seeing him again, dear?'

'Yes. He's invited me to a tennis party at his house.'

'No need for you to be nervous about that,' her mother said confidently. 'You're a better player than most people.'

'I'm over my nerves now, Mum. I'll be fine.'

'I was thinking… Easter is coming up next week. The whole family will be here as usual. Why not invite Ethan to come to Sunday lunch?'

A vision of her family swarming around him, prob-ably assuming things about their relationship they shouldn't assume and making stomach-squirming com-ments, played havoc with the nerves she had just de-clared in fine condition.

'I think it's too soon for that,' she said, inwardly recoiling from any move that might bring rejection and the crushing of a dream that she hoped might come true, given enough solid time together.

'It would be a nice way of showing our appreciation for what he's done for us,' her mother pressed.

'Mum, it was business,' Daisy said emphatically. 'Ethan would have been rewarded for it, taking a commission on the deal.' Her cheeks burned. She couldn't look at him.

'But that's so impersonal, Daisy,' her mother argued. 'And what he did was personal. It was because he was pleased with you. You told us so yourself. And it's obvious he's still pleased with you. Ask him if he'd like to come.'

Daisy gritted her teeth and thought hard. 'He probably has family of his own to go to at Easter.'

'Well, if he has, he has. There's no harm in extending an invitation.'

'Okay. I'll let you know.' Please, God, let her stop now, Daisy prayed.

She didn't.

'You'll be coming home anyway, won't you, dear? We haven't seen you since you took up your new job.'

Her free time was exclusively Ethan's. That was the deal. But surely he'd understand she had to attend the family get-together at Easter. 'Yes, I'll be there,' she answered unequivocally, not wanting to make some excuse unless she was forced to.

'It will be such a happy day,' her mother rattled on. 'Ken and Kevin are both employed again. Your father has paid off Keith's business debts, and we can now afford to send Violet's boy to a special school for autistic children.'

'That's great!'

It really was—alleviating a lot of stress in her sister's

life. Money was not the root of all evil, Daisy thought. It could be a huge blessing.

'Well, I'll let you go, dear, but do ask Ethan if he'd like to join us for Easter Sunday. He'll be most welcome. Such a handsome man, too,' she added in a tone overflowing with benevolence, causing Daisy to fly into a panic.

'Mum, don't get ideas. This was a first date, remember. It doesn't *mean* anything.'

'Of course it does, Daisy. It means that he likes you and you like him. Now don't do anything to spoil it, dear. I thought you looked perfect together. Bye now.'

Daisy fumbled the receiver's return to its cradle, dropped back down on the pillow and closed her eyes. Tight. To shut out the dreadful embarrassment of knowing Ethan had overheard that conversation and had undoubtedly pieced together her mother's side of it.

She felt him shift onto his side, prop himself up to examine the expression on her face, felt his eyes probing under her skin. A featherlight finger teased one corner of her mouth. 'It doesn't *mean* anything?'

For some reason his repetition of those words hurt unbearably. She opened her eyes and attacked with defensive ferocity. 'You know perfectly well why I'm here with you, Ethan. Just because you've taken me out of your closet hasn't changed the deal, has it?'

He frowned. 'Weren't you happy with me today?'

'That's not the point! My parents saw the presentation of The Golden Slipper on TV, saw us together, and my mother has leapt to the rosy conclusion that we're a match made in heaven.'

His mouth quirked in amusement. 'Maybe we are.'

'Don't make fun of it!' she cried, hope giving her

heart a painful kick. 'I have to deal with this now. My family always get together at my parents' home at Easter. They'll be full of questions about you and...' Her eyes pleaded to be let off his hook. 'I know you demanded all my free time, but I'll be breaking our family tradition if I'm not there with them.'

'No problem.' His eyes glinted with determined purpose. 'I'll go with you.'

She stared at him, her stomach curdling at the thought of what he'd be walking into. 'I'm only asking for one day with my family, Ethan. Not even one full day. Lunch on Easter Sunday will be enough.'

'Fine!' he said. 'We'll roll up for lunch on Easter Sunday.'

Daisy closed her eyes again as she tried to swallow the sickening surge of panic. There was no moving him. He was bent on having his own way, relentlessly ruthless about getting it.

'Your mother did invite me, didn't she?' he said without any doubt in his voice.

'Yes,' she bit out between gritted teeth.

'Then tell her I accept.'

Daisy summoned up one last effort to change his mind, shooting him a begging look. 'We're a big family, Ethan. And because I've never brought anyone into it, they'll pepper you with questions and size you up like you wouldn't believe.'

She had invited Carl when she'd believed in their love for each other, but he had always found some pressing reason not to be available when she'd wanted him to accompany her. From the arguments preceding their break-up, she'd realised he resented her family and the hold it had on her, taking her away from what he wanted to do. If Ethan also resented their claim on her...

'It won't worry me, Daisy,' he said, obviously not caring about being put in a hot seat. 'I'm curious about them, too. I'll enjoy meeting such a close-knit family. I haven't had one myself.'

She heaved a resigned sigh. He was resolved on accompanying her, no matter what. She could only hope he did enjoy himself and somehow, miraculously, feel he could become a part of her family because there was no long-term future with him if he couldn't.

The week slipped by all too quickly.

Daisy's emotions were worn ragged, fretting over how her family would receive Ethan and vice versa.

He peppered her with questions about them, memorising all the names and connecting the children to the right parents, doing his homework before making an entrance. Applying good business practice, Daisy thought, but meeting a diverse group of people whose life experiences were nothing like his was much more complex than sitting down with a bunch of clients with similar interests—namely big money and what to do with it. She remembered how she'd hated him for being what he was—obscenely rich, stunningly handsome and sinfully sexy. Her brothers and sister could feel the same way.

It did alleviate a little of her inner stress when he showed a particular interest in Joshua, Violet's autistic son. She explained that he didn't seem to relate to people at all. It was as though he was locked into a world of his own and he was obsessed with numbers, always counting everything. It was important to simply accept this, not treat him as odd, and Ethan assured her he understood.

But he didn't understand what he was walking into. She had to stop him from buying a huge basket of chocolate Easter bunnies and eggs for the children. Their parents, who couldn't afford such expensive luxuries, might resent such largesse, although she couldn't bring herself to tell him so, saying only she'd be taking a bag of little Easter eggs to be hidden in the garden for the treasure hunt, and too much was too much. It would be enough if he gave her mother a box of chocolates as a thank-you gift.

The family day loomed as a nightmare.

She had no happy dreams about it at all.

In fact, she was fairly certain it would end the dream she had been nursing.

She and Ethan came from different worlds which were too far apart to bridge the gap. Common sense had told her that this was an ill-fated attraction, leading only to bed while lust was running hot. She should have stayed in the closet for the rest of this year—deal done and free to run. That wouldn't have raised any family problems and she wouldn't be feeling so horribly torn, wanting the impossible.

Ethan was acutely aware of Daisy's tension over this coming visit with her family. He gradually came to realise she didn't believe he could fit into her world. Proving to her that she could fit into his only resolved half the problem that had made her keep him at a distance until he'd forced her into a relationship with him.

She hadn't come into it feeling it was right for her. She'd done it for her family. That close-knit unit meant more to her than anything else and Ethan was beginning to sense he had to win acceptance and liking from every one of them to free Daisy of her misgivings about their connection.

This was a completely foreign situation to him. He'd been more or less detached from his parents since boyhood. While he was quite fond of both of them, they played absolutely no part in his relationships with other people. That was his personal business, nothing to do with them. He didn't seek their approval. They never showed disapproval. The decisions were his. He was the one who had to live with them. That had been drummed into him for as long as he could remember.

This definitely was not the case with Daisy. How he reacted to her family and how they responded to him was obviously a huge issue in her mind. He'd met her father and liked him, but money had been the only agenda at those meetings, not his daughter.

All he knew for certain was he had another battle on his hands.

And Daisy was worth fighting for.

CHAPTER FIFTEEN

'MY BROTHERS always wear jeans,' Daisy told Ethan before he dressed on Sunday morning.

He obligingly took the hint and dressed in jeans.

'It's better if we go in my car,' she said as they were about to leave.

The green eyes turned hard and resolute. 'There's no hiding who I am, Daisy.'

True, but he didn't have to rub their noses in his wealth with a flash BMW. She returned a challenging look. 'This is a first meeting. Do you want my family to see you or your car?'

It was a major test, and to Daisy's intense relief, Ethan acknowledged her point. 'Okay, we'll go in yours.' His mouth quirked in wry appeal. 'Will that help you relax?'

She heaved a sigh to loosen up the tightness in her chest and managed a wobbly smile. 'I can't help feeling a bit anxious. I want them to like you.'

He smiled back, taking her hand and squeezing it. 'I want that, too.'

It lifted some of the burden from her heart. As she drove them both to Ryde, she kept telling herself Ethan had shown himself master of any situation and he would handle this one as well as he'd handled the barbecue with the tradesmen. However, that wasn't really the problem. If their relationship was to have any chance of a long future, this visit would be the first of many, not a single occasion that could be easily negotiated. The big question was whether he would want to repeat the experience or prefer to back off from it.

She parked her car in the street adjacent to the one where her parents lived. 'Which house?' Ethan asked, eyeing the nearby residences.

They were all ordinary brick houses, as was her parents', their architecture very basic. Nevertheless, it was a good, friendly neighbourhood, neat, tidy, gardens well tended, and Daisy was not about to apologise for its lack of class. This was where she came from and where she would come back to if Ethan couldn't accept it.

'Not here,' she answered. 'Around the corner. Our house is in a cul-de-sac and all the children will be out playing street cricket. I don't want the car to be in their way. It's not far to walk.'

'Street cricket?' Ethan looked bemused.

'It's a family tradition. Every Easter Sunday morning.' She nodded to her brothers who'd spotted her car and were waving at them. 'That's Ken and Kevin standing on the corner, watching out for any incoming traffic and fielding any long balls anyone hits.'

'Sounds like fun. Can I join in?'

'If you want to. Though you'll need to meet everyone first. Mum and Violet and my sisters-in-law will be in the kitchen preparing lunch.'

They alighted from the car and Daisy watched her

brothers eyeing Ethan over as they walked up to meet them. They were older than him, in their forties, and they were both grinning as though they were happy to see their baby sister with a man in tow. They made the introductions easy, warmly welcoming Ethan and calling out to the children to say 'Hi!' to their aunt Daisy and her friend. The game was briefly interrupted for yelled greetings and clamours for Ethan to play with them after he'd said hello to Nan and Pop.

There was no awkward hitch in any of the introductions. Ethan impressed everyone with already knowing their names and enough about them to strike up a friendly conversation. When her father led him out of the kitchen to join the street game, her mother gave Daisy a big hug, declaring him a lovely man.

'He is a bit much, though,' Violet commented with a worried look. 'What I mean is…he must be used to women falling all over him and getting his own way. Be careful about giving him your heart, Daisy. He might not be good husband material.'

'That was part of why I was reluctant to become involved with him,' she confided, understanding precisely what her sister meant. 'But the more I've come to know him, the more I like him, Violet. Not for his wealth or his good looks. They were stumbling blocks to me, too. I don't know where this relationship is going. I just like being with him. Okay?'

'Okay.' She smiled and raised her hand. 'Fingers crossed that it works out fine for you. Now tell us more about him.'

Daisy carefully chose to give what she thought was sympathetic information, concentrating on Ethan's family background—parents wrapped up in their academic careers, how he learned to love cooking from his grandmother, being sent to boarding school, his pleasure in games. It seemed to satisfy the general curiosity and gave a more rounded view of the person he was.

Her mother was roasting the traditional leg of pork with all the trimmings. The men had already set up a long trestle table in the family room with the twenty-four chairs needed to seat everyone, and as the women chatted, they did all the settings with colourful Easter motif serviettes and bon-bons. The centrepiece was a large round white chocolate mud-cake with a hole in the middle which was filled in and piled high with brightly wrapped miniature Easter eggs. They mixed a fruit punch for the children and put out wineglasses for the adults. It all looked wonderfully festive and Daisy hoped Ethan would enjoy what was always a rowdy luncheon with her family.

She slipped out to the back garden and hid her Easter eggs for the treasure hunt before the children trooped inside from the street. When everything was done and ready they called everyone in to clean up and sit down, which they did in high good humour. From comments flying around, Ethan had endeared himself to the children by hitting lollipop catches when he was batting, and the easiest to hit balls when he was bowling. Masterly control, Daisy thought, and was pleased he'd applied it to make the game more fun.

She actually started to relax over lunch. Ethan happily joined in the many topics of conversation raised, though he listened more than he talked. He complimented her mother on the pork crackling—the best he'd ever eaten. He laughed at her brothers' jokes. He really seemed to be having a good time.

After the cake had been served and eaten, the children were allowed to leave the table and go on the treasure hunt. They leapt from their chairs excitedly, eager to add to their hoard of chocolate—all except Joshua, who remained seated, counting and recounting his share of eggs from the cake. Violet left her seat to coax him into joining the others. He ignored her efforts and when she took him by the hand, he lashed out, hitting her arm to leave him alone, then flying into a major tantrum, screaming and throwing a flurry of punches at her.

They were all used to this kind of sudden eruption from him, but Violet was upset and embarrassed that it was happening in front of Ethan, breaking into tears and throwing them a helpless look of despair at her inability to control her autistic son. Her husband, Barry, rushed to her side, swooped on Joshua, lifted him up to his shoulder and carried him out of the room.

'I'm sorry…sorry,' Violet cried, covering her face with her hands.

Her mother enveloped her in a hug, patting her back and speaking soothingly, 'Don't take on so, dear. We all understand.'

'It's spoiled the day for Daisy,' she wailed.

'No, it hasn't,' Daisy insisted, going to her sister to add her comfort. If Ethan was put off by a child with a condition that sometimes defied control, then so be it. No family was perfect, but it was a poor family that didn't give each other support when it was needed.

To her astonishment, Ethan joined her, appealing to her sister in a gentle voice. 'Would you mind if I tried something that might interest Joshua, Violet, calm him down?'

'Oh, dear God, what?' she cried.

He whipped what looked like a slim black notebook from his shirt pocket. 'Look! It's a Nintendo brain-trainer. Daisy told me Joshua was fascinated by numbers. I can bring up a program that might catch his attention. How about you take me to him and we can give it a go?'

Violet shook her head at him in wonderment. Daisy, too, was amazed at his initiative. Her mother took charge. 'Go on, Violet. Give Ethan a chance of focussing Joshua's interest on something.'

'All right,' she answered dazedly, and led him off to the bedroom wing.

Daisy and her mother started clearing the table, needing to do something. The rest of the adults left their chairs to help.

'You've got a good guy there, Daisy,' Ken commented approvingly.

'He was great with the other kids, too,' Kevin remarked.

She flushed with pleasure in their liking of Ethan, though she felt constrained to warn them it might not be a serious relationship. 'We haven't been together long,' she started.

'You don't have to be to know you've found someone special,' her mother slid in with an arch look.

'Yes, I wouldn't be letting him go in a hurry, Daisy,' Keith's wife tagged on.

'Rope him in and nail him down,' Keith advised with a grin.

They all laughed, though Daisy couldn't help thinking they were missing the point. There was no question that Ethan was special. The problem was whether she was special enough for him. He was certainly making an extraordinary effort to draw her family onside with him. If he managed to pull Joshua into a state of contentment again, he'd be the hero of the day.

Her mother had opened Ethan's gift box of chocolates and put it on the table for everyone to help themselves and they were just sitting down again to relax over cups of coffee when the three missing adults returned with smiles on their faces.

'I can't believe it!' Violet crowed happily. 'Ethan showed Joshua how to do Sudoku puzzles on that Nintendo gadget and he's enthralled with it.'

'Problem is, he won't want to give it back, Ethan,' Barry said ruefully. 'If you tell me how much it cost, I'll pay you for it.'

'No, please…I'm happy for him to keep it.'

Barry shook his head. 'Can't let you do that.'

'To tell you the truth, I didn't buy it for me. I bought it for him, Barry.'

There was a moment of stunned silence.

Ethan shot Daisy an ironic grimace, then explained how he'd come to do it. 'I'd already made the purchase before Daisy said I wasn't to bring gifts for the children. She'd told me about Joshua's fascination with numbers and it struck a chord with me because numbers have always played a big part in my life. Anyhow, I slipped it into my pocket, just in case the opportunity came up to share a game with him. I honestly have no use for it, myself.'

More silence that sent prickles all the way down Daisy's spine.

This was the kind of buying-power thing she'd wanted to avoid—obvious evidence of how easily Ethan could acquire anything, cost no object.

The expensive gift could hurt Barry's paternal pride.

It could instantly undermine the liking Ethan had earned earlier, making her family see him as the big-shot financier, intent on buying himself into their midst, so wealthy himself he was beyond empathising with the difficulties they'd faced and were still facing though their situations had improved. Partly because of him.

Although a gift could be welcomed out of sheer need, the giver could be deeply resented. Daisy was painfully aware of how negatively she had reacted to Ethan until she'd come to know him.

Violet broke the uncomfortable impasse. 'That's very thoughtful of you, Ethan. Very kind,' she said appreciatively.

'Yes,' Barry backed her up, grimacing over his own lack of understanding of his son as he added, 'I've always found Joshua's fixation on numbers weird. I would never have connected it to a game he could play.' He clapped Ethan on the shoulder. 'I'm glad you did. It might be a step forward for him.'

They were smoothing over his gaffe in not accepting Barry's offer to pay.

The iron fist squeezing Daisy's heart eased its grip.

Ethan gestured an apologetic appeal to the rest of the family. 'I hope the other children won't mind him having it.'

'Not at all,' Ken replied cheerfully. 'They'll be too busy feeding their faces with chocolate. Like us. The three of you had better sit down and indulge yourselves before we polish off this whole decadent box you brought for Mum.'

'If you've scoffed all the ones with caramel fillings, Ken, I'll scalp you,' Violet threatened, quickly coming to look.

'Haven't got enough hair left to worry about,' he retorted, grinning evilly at her.

Everyone laughed and Daisy's pent-up tension was finally expelled. Ethan resumed his seat beside her and she gave his hand a quick squeeze, grateful for what he'd done for Joshua and relieved that no one seemed to be holding his generosity against him, not on the surface anyway. What they thought privately would probably never be discussed in her hearing. She could only hope that his kindness overrode any niggles about the gift.

The party mood was quickly re-established.

Daisy relaxed again.

Keith opened a bottle of champagne and insisted they all have a glass of it because he had things to say and people to toast. Her oldest brother enjoyed making speeches, which were always amusing, so as Keith took his stand, glass in hand, Daisy was smiling in anticipation, not expecting the tenor of this speech to be different today.

'This past year has been a difficult one for all of us. It's great to have it behind us with better times to look forward to,' he started seriously, drawing murmurs of agreement from around the table.

'The first toast I want to make is to our baby sister. The rest of us were not in a position to help Mum and Dad when they needed it, and Daisy took up the slack like the little champion she is. We all think the world of you for contributing all you did, Daisy, and if there's anything we can ever do for you, you have only to ask.'

More murmurs of agreement.

Daisy flushed with embarrassed pleasure. While it was lovely to have her resolute support of their parents appreciated, she couldn't help wondering if her family had gone out of their way to welcome Ethan just to make her happy. It fitted with Violet's distressed cry about spoiling her day. Was there genuine liking for him or an act put on for her sake?

'To Daisy,' Keith went on.

They all toasted her.

'Next, I want to thank Ethan for taking on Dad's investments and giving him his expert advice, turning what looked like a black hole into a gold mine.' He grinned at Ethan. 'That was a real bonanza, and for us to see the worry lifted from Mum's and Dad's faces, to see them enjoying life again…you've done us all a power of good, Ethan. We salute you.'

They all raised their glasses again to toast him.

Ethan frowned, shifting uncomfortably, then lifted a hand in protest at the toast. 'No, I can't accept that, Keith. What I did… I wasn't thinking of your parents or this family. I didn't know you.' He shot a wry smile at Daisy. 'It was to hold onto this woman, to win more time with her, because I wanted her in my life and she was walking out of it.'

'Well, we did think there was a bit of self-interest involved,' Keith said dryly. 'But that doesn't alter the fact that you changed everything around for Mum and Dad and you deserve some acknowledgement for it.'

'Then let me acknowledge something, too,' Ethan swiftly put in. 'Now that I've been amongst you, I see more clearly why Daisy is the very special person she is. Being an only child myself, I haven't had your experience of family, but today I've learnt why it means so much to her. You all share something very special. It's what I'd love to have in my own life, and I'm hoping

Daisy...' he turned to her, his green eyes glittering with determination '...will want to make it happen with me.'

Daisy was totally stunned.

Was he saying what she thought he was saying?

Making a family of their own?

Marriage...children?

Her heart broke out of its suspended state of shock and started to gallop.

"Right!' she heard Keith say. 'Got to agree our little sister is special and we're glad you recognise it, Ethan. Makes you special, too. Seems like a good idea if you two wander off to the front porch or behind a bush along the side fence and talk about what you want together while we clear this table for some serious poker.'

Seize the day...the thought had instantly leapt into Ethan's mind.

Keith had just given him the family's stamp of approval. That barrier in Daisy's mind had to be down. If he acted now, before she could get herself in a twist about something else, he should be able to clinch the real deal.

'Yes. Good idea!' he shot at Keith with a huge man-to-man grin.

He grabbed Daisy's hand, pulled her up from her chair, and swept her out to the front porch, his heart drumming him into the battle he was intent on winning. The moment the door was closed behind them, ensuring privacy, he scooped her hard against him, one arm curling possessively around her waist, his free hand cupping her chin so she couldn't look away from the intensity of purpose shooting from his eyes to hers.

'There's no more to prove, is there?' he fiercely challenged. Without waiting for a reply he plunged on with vehement conviction. 'We're fine together, Daisy. Doesn't matter who we're with or where we are. The world is our oyster if you'll just open up to me and admit that I'm the right man for you. The right man in every respect. Because I am. I know it. And you're the right woman for me. No question. We could build a great future together. Have a family like yours. Nothing should stop us. Nothing!'

The right woman for him...

He meant it.

It was in his voice, in his eyes, and at last Daisy could let herself believe it. All the doubts that had plagued her disintegrated under the forcefulness of Ethan's insistent claims. A huge welling of emotion brought tears to her eyes. She couldn't speak. She flung her arms around his neck and kissed him, pouring into passion the hopes and dreams he had just turned into incredibly ecstatic reality.

He *was* the right man for her. In every respect. Her heart and soul told her so, and her body exulted in the passion he returned with its promise of always being there for her—no time limit—for the rest of their lives, not the rest of this year.

'Now that *meant* something,' he muttered with certainty as his mouth broke from hers.

A sublime joy bubbled into laughter. Her eyes danced total agreement with him as she sobered up enough to say, 'I love you, Ethan Cartwright. I just didn't know if *you'd* ever think we'd be fine together.'

'Thought it from the first day we met,' he answered, his eyes sparkling with delight in her open admission.

'You didn't even know me,' she protested.

'Knew it instinctively. Convincing *you* of it was the problem.'

She shook her head at him. 'You only wanted me.'

'Very badly. And once I had you, Daisy Donahue, I very quickly knew I never wanted to let you go. I love everything about you. Absolutely everything.'

It was what she had secretly yearned to hear and it was happening.

It truly was.

Ethan cocked an eyebrow enquiringly. 'Does your father expect me to ask him for your hand in marriage?'

'You haven't asked *me* yet,' she reminded him.

He laughed. 'Shall I go down on bended knee?'

'No, I like you better up here,' she said, swaying her body provocatively against his, revelling in the freedom of being able to express her love for him without any inhibitions at all.

'Will you…' he kissed her forehead '…be…' he kissed the tip of her nose '…my wife?' He brushed his lips over hers.

'Yes,' she breathed against his mouth and they kissed again, celebrating the soul-deep satisfaction of knowing they were, indeed, right for each other.

They stayed out on the front porch for quite a while, not wanting to break the marvellous sense of solid to-getherness. It seemed to Daisy they had come on a long, long journey to this point, and there was much to talk about—the inner turmoil that had constantly infiltrated her part in their relationship, the moves Ethan had made to give himself the best chance of winning her over to what he wanted, the reasons why he'd decided she was the right woman for him, his realisation that her integrity was rock-solid, that there was no intention of *taking* him for anything beyond what had been agreed—so many feelings to be expressed, explained, understood.

And a future to be planned.

Ethan wanted to fill the house at Hunters Hill with children, to play games with them, to sit down to family meals, which matched Daisy's dreams perfectly. They would make it happen together. They were one in mind, one in heart—soul mates for ever.

It was the most blissful day in Daisy's life and, wonderfully imbued with the absolute confidence he gave her, she knew with Ethan there would be many more to come.

He did ask her father for her hand in marriage.

In front of the whole family.

And their response made the day even better—nothing but genuine, heart-warming pleasure for both of them all around.

Easter Sunday…

Not a nightmare.

A dream come true.

Coming Next Month

in **Harlequin Presents® EXTRA.** Available September 14, 2010.

Coming Next Month

in **Harlequin Presents®.** Available September 28, 2010.

LARGER-PRINT BOOKS!

*See below for a sneak peek at
our inspirational line, Love Inspired®.
Introducing HIS HOLIDAY BRIDE
by bestselling author Jillian Hart*

Autumn Granger gave her horse rein to slide toward the town's new sheriff.

"Hey, there." The man in a brand-new Stetson, black T-shirt, jeans and riding boots held up a hand in greeting. He stepped away from his four-wheel drive with "Sheriff" in black on the doors and waded through the grasses. "I'm new around here."

"I'm Autumn Granger."

"Nice to meet you, Miss Granger. I'm Ford Sherman, from Chicago." He knuckled back his hat, revealing the most handsome face she'd ever seen. Big blue eyes contrasted with his sun-tanned complexion.

"I'm guessing you haven't seen much open land. Out here, you've got to keep an eye on cows or they're going to tear your vehicle apart."

"What?" He whipped around. Sure enough, mammoth black-and-white creatures had started to gnaw on his four-wheel drive. They clustered like a mob, mouths and tongues and teeth bent on destruction. One cow tried to pry the wiper off the windshield, another chewed on the side mirror. Several leaned through the open window, licking the seats.

"Move along, little dogie." He didn't know the first thing about cattle.

The entire herd swiveled their heads to study him curiously. Not a single hoof shifted. The animals soon returned to chewing, licking, digging through his possessions.

Autumn laughed, a warm and wonderful sound. "Thanks,

I needed that." She then pulled a bag from behind her saddle and waved it at the cows. "Look what I have, guys. Cookies."

Cows swung in her direction, and dozens of liquid brown eyes brightened with cookie hopes. As she circled the car, the cattle bounded after her. The earth shook with the force of their powerful hooves.

"Next time, you're on your own, city boy." She tipped her hat. The cowgirl stayed on his mind, the sweetest thing he had ever seen.

*Will Ford be able to stick it out in the country
to find out more about Autumn?
Find out in HIS HOLIDAY BRIDE
by bestselling author Jillian Hart,
available in October 2010
only from Love Inspired®.*